THE LAST MISTRESS OF JOSE RIZAL

The Last Mistress of Jose Rizal

STORIES

Brian Ascalon Roley

CURBSTONE BOOKS
NORTHWESTERN UNIVERSITY PRESS
EVANSTON, ILLINOIS

Northwestern University Press
www.nupress.northwestern.edu

Printed in the United States of America

10 9 8 7 6 5 4 3 2 1

ISBN 978-0-8101-3322-8 (paper)
ISBN 978-0-8101-3323-5 (e-book)

This is a work of fiction. Characters, places, and events are the product of the author's imagination or are used fictitiously and do not represent actual people, places, or events.

Library of Congress Cataloging-in-Publication Data
Names: Roley, Brian Ascalon, author.
Title: The last mistress of Jose Rizal : stories / Brian Ascalon Roley.
Other titles: Short stories. English
Description: Evanston, Illinois : Curbstone Books : Northwestern University Press, 2016.
Identifiers: LCCN 2015044031 | ISBN 9780810133228 (pbk. : alk. paper) | ISBN 9780810133235 (ebook)
Subjects: LCSH: Filipino American families—Fiction.
Classification: LCC PS3568.O5333 A6 2016 | DDC 813.6—dc23 LC record available at http://lccn.loc.gov/2015044031

For Gwen, Brendan, Aidan, and Family

CONTENTS

Part One

Part Two

THE LAST MISTRESS OF JOSE RIZAL

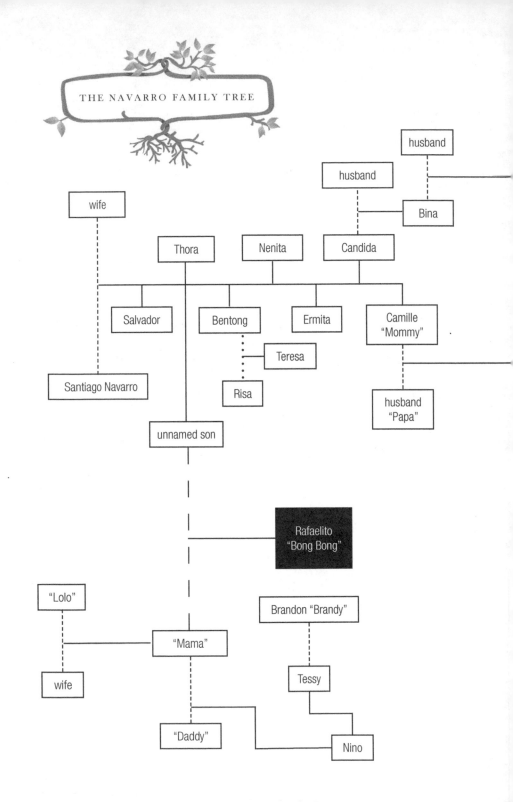

THE NAVARRO FAMILY TREE

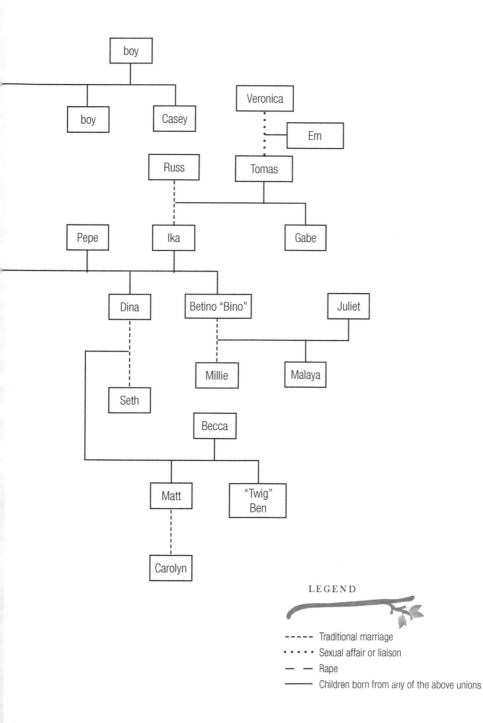

LEGEND

- - - - - Traditional marriage
• • • • • Sexual affair or liaison
— — Rape
——— Children born from any of the above unions

Part One

The Last Mistress of Jose Rizal

I wish to tell my daughter Bina, you are a great-great-grandniece of Jose Rizal, poet, novelist, revolutionary, martyr, a surgeon in Europe, and a linguist in nineteen languages living and three dead—ancient Sanskrit and Greek and Latin—and he had six mistresses in six different countries, the portraits of whom you can see in many restaurants in metro Manila, and you will see his name on every main street and on the side of every jeepney. This is your heritage. Your heritage is an ancient and schooled tradition. In my childhood we girls spoke Spanish in the home and in school with the quick flavor of Castile. We had money then to send our daughters to finishing school in Salamanca. The men studied at Padua, Oxford, Santo Tomas, Ateneo de Manila, and France.

Then we had money, and we squandered it. Jose Rizal had no children so you, by way of his sister, are as true an heir to his tradition as any. When you were a child I took you to the monument to his greatness, the former Spanish colonial Fort Santiago, and you saw the Rizal museum where they had put up a family chart of his descendants, outside an old stone soldiers' barracks, and you excitedly pointed to where your name is written there. Yet now you are here and married to this American man and living in a dilapidated farmhouse in Illinois. I cannot understand this. Also in our tradition is a noble and ancient Catholic Church and my understanding has always been that the wife is in charge of her children's spiritual growth. This man says he is a Christian, and it is nice how he spends much time with your children, but I can't understand this place you call a church. When I first walked inside, on that first Sunday I came to live with you and your "Christian" husband, as he so often calls himself, the first thing I saw was not a great mosaic, not a statue of the Blessed Mother, not even a humble carving of one of the ancient saints–no, the first thing I noticed was that at the place where the ceiling meets the wall there is a crack, and from this I could discern that it was drywall. You could see the plaster beneath the thin layer of paint. It smelled of new carpet. The hall was thick with these farm people, many wearing jeans, and in the hall of prayer I saw no altar nor crucifix but merely a simple wooden cross, before which some young people set their guitars and microphones and a drum set and began playing "Christian music." This went on for half an hour. I kept waiting for the service to begin–for the creeds or prayers–but I finally realized that this was their service. I have listened to Georgian chants in monasteries in Italy, and even Eastern chants deep in the heart of Russia, and I can tell you this was not what I expected. You will forgive me if I tell you I was disappointed when the minister finally came onstage; this man with his ill-fitted suit, broad shoulders, and hickish hair cut short over the ears and let long in back, gave one the impression that he was a shoe salesman, though he did seem friendly.

I would like to tell my daughter that her husband was curt with me the other day. But of course I cannot say this. It is best if I do not. I have tried not to be an ungrateful guest and this is his farm, I know, and these are his children–but I do not see that I did anything wrong, and it has always been my understanding the mother's family is the one that provides guidance on religion. My daughter's husband, this man, he came to me yesterday when I was on the porch in the morning in prayer. It was early and the sun not yet risen, although the air was warm and thick. But a breeze blew through the corn and it reminded me of my father's plantation of my youth–Kawayan–also known as Navarro, my maiden name. This was before I had a daughter, or any children, and we ran through the coconut trees whose fronds shook of the wind an hour to the ocean. There was a chapel there, and we prayed. It was a simple peasant's hut, made of fronds, with simple dolls of the saints put in by the peasants. This was enough for us, then. So I don't see how this man who is my daughter's husband can call Catholics idol worshipers. A hut was enough for us. My granddaughter came up to me on the porch that morning. She asked me if I was an idol worshiper. I said *no*. She said her father's friend said he prayed for my soul. He said she should pray with him, to get on her knees.

I said, You do not have to pray for my soul, Casey. I'm not an idol worshiper.

Mr. Baker said if I love you, I should.

Don't worry for me, Casey. He is wrong.

But she retained that worried look in her eyes, with her head cocked sideways as if she was not sure whether she believed me.

So I decided to show her the picture book with the photos of French cathedrals, Saint Peter's in Rome, the Basilica; also paintings of Michelangelo, Raphael, and Goya. Such things could not be made but with the inspiration of God, I explained to her. Casey regarded me with her eyes—hazelnut from her father's side—looking worried; and she wore ill-fitted jeans like a boy and a tank top shirt like the peasants on my father's farm. These were even dirty. I wished I could buy her a dress, but I couldn't. I felt sorry and so had her fetch my picture book. It was a moment of sentiment, yes. A slight error, as I had promised my daughter's husband I would not show it. But she looked so plain in her clothes. Like the peasants in the farm—and even wealthy youth in Manila, who dress like teenagers in American shows. And though it is fine when you are in Manila to admire some things American, it is also nice for a Filipino child in America to know something of her heritage.

Casey flipped the thick pages. I didn't tell her to, she began flipping herself. The cathedrals looked nice in the rose light of the predawn, strangely made soft by the nearness of so many corn fronds. A cathedral would look nice on this farm. It is plain, plain, plain. And was it not nice for me to show her that our native religion was greatness, not idolatry? As rightful as I felt, when I heard the screen door creak open and rattle shut, I felt in my body a quick jolt of worry, which has been so pronounced since I have lived on this continent, and heard his thick heavy footsteps approach. The porch moved. It seemed to sink. I felt his body standing above me, and he leaned forward and took my book.

From his shadow's movement I knew he opened its cover, and searched the pages. He did not give it back. I bought this book from a small Italian bookshop while on a trip to the Vatican, in a narrow hillside alleyway in Rome.

I had inserted a scrap portrait into this book of Josephine Bracken, an Irish woman, Jose Rizal's favorite and final mistress; it was pressed within the last pages. My deceased brother Bentong had given it to me, and I wanted to show it to Casey. I hope it does not get lost.

This man who is my daughter's husband, I watch him leave for the fields in the mornings, from my wicker chair on the porch, and all day have to watch my grandchildren do chores around the house like the peasants—like simple people—even the girl, Casey, who will turn out like a boy unless I can do something about it—and I tell you it is a strange thing to watch your granddaughter hauling buckets of horse manure about, with its stink and swarm of flies. She would look very pretty in a floral dress. A Spanish dress, like the girls of Salamanca. With my blood and his American blood she looks beautifully Spanish, and whoever heard of a Spanish girl going to a church whose floor is industrial carpet? For pews they have foldable chairs. At their entrance they have a desk with a sign that says VISITORS and a man standing behind it all smiling like a concierge. Candida Navarro, I thought to myself. This place is a hotel, not a place of worship.

The boys I do not like. They are rough and pale looking. The little one is disrespectful. The older one is ugly. They tell their friends I am a Mexican and have stolen my rosaries. Their friends laugh.

But this girl has the blood of Jose Rizal. When she is upset with her mother—when her ears go red, and she squeezes her fists and I hear the little shoes stomping away from her mother—I know she has the poet's blood. She comes to my room, when she is angry, and sleeps in my bed. I hold her hand, and although once her tiny fingers would have fit into the palm of mine, now my fingers are thin from age, and our fingers twine nicely together. Her blood beats quickly, warmly in the tips. I teach her the rosary. She knows the Mysteries by heart.

She says, Why do they call them Mysteries?

I stroke the warm drops of sweat that soak her little forehead: Because this is a strange world which operates according to laws we do not understand. It is not in us to understand His ways.

She ponders this, and nods her head. It is the poet Rizal in her, I sense. I feel a quick fluttering in my chest, just to think of this. Like a butterfly within my heart. Even in her Spanishness she bears a marked resemblance to the poet's last and most beautiful mistress, Josephine Bracken, an Irish woman whose portrait you can see in many fine restaurants in Manila. She is not related, but the resemblance is there. I tell my granddaughter, You must be careful.

Why? she says.

You have the poet's blood.

There. I put the word to it. In our family it has become almost taboo to say such a thing. To have the poet's blood is both a good and a dangerous matter. Jose Rizal's blood beat quickly in anger, and he wrote against the treatment of our country by the Spanish, and for this he was martyred in his thirties. He wrote many beautiful poems but lived in sin outside the Catholic Church. In our family we have those who have accomplished many things in this life, like Rizal the doctor. But there are others, like my sisters Nenita and Ernita and Thora, and perhaps all but a handful of my uncles and brothers, who are brilliant and lost and have taken to drinking and anger and wandering the world.

What is the poet's blood? the girl says.

Some of your uncles have had it. They have killed men and led guerrilla armies. The jungles about our hacienda are peopled with their illegitimate children. Others accomplished much good in this life. Doctors. Attorneys. Businessmen. Priests. All have the blood of Jose Rizal. His face is on our country's money.

What is an illegitimate children?

I do not answer her. You must be very careful, I say.

Why?

It is a hard life. *Ay Buhay, Dios ko po*, we have these sayings. But you are beautiful like Josephine Bracken. That is both good and dangerous.

She wants to know what Josephine Bracken looks like, and I tell her about the picture in the book her father took away. I know I shouldn't have. She looks at me strangely, then says she will ask her father to give it back.

No.

But it's your picture.

Let's not make trouble, Casey.

She frowns, but I tell her again not to mention this to her father. After all, if he is going to give my photo back, he should do it on his own.

But the next morning I find the picture book set on the wicker table on the porch, beneath a crumpling of musty newspapers. I lift the sheets aside, and it is there, the clear cover lightly dusty. Within the book I see that the picture of Rizal's final mistress is gone, and I know Casey has it and it was she who had gone to her father. She disobeyed me. I look for her with my eyes, but all that morning she does not pass in front of the porch. Then, after noon, I see her cross from the back of the barn and take the long way to enter by the side of the house, her gaze shyly avoiding my direction.

I shout, *Casey!* but she pretends not to hear.

Finally, when the sun has lowered over the fields so that it comes softly through the waved and crooked screen, as through warped and crooked glass, she steps shyly into the doorway from the house. I call her over.

Casey, I say. You should not have told your father.

I didn't.

I told you not to tell him.

I didn't tell him.

Don't lie to me, Casey. I know you put the book here on the table. Didn't you?

She says that she did but that she took the book without telling her father.

I grip her hand and pull her close to me. Casey.

What?

Put it back.

She does not want to. Within her fingers is clutched the withered portrait of Josephine Bracken, who does indeed look like Casey. It has been a long time since I have looked at this picture. I am sure of it now, she has the poet's blood. I feel a chill in my old bones. She hides it behind her back, her ears going red again with indignation.

Give me the picture, I say.

Why?

Now, I say.

She tells me it is mine and not her father's. It is not stealing.

I clutch her again, closer. I hold her wrists and feel the sharpness of her American bones. I tell her she must be extra careful not to be sinful; to be vigilant, to look after her soul.

After she leaves to return the picture to her father, I worry about her soul. The sun sets and shadows lengthen and vanish, but still I worry. My daughter comes out and calls me to dinner, but I am too busy praying. She hesitates in the doorway, then leaves. An hour later she tries again, but I am in a Hail Mary.

That night I pray. I do not sleep or eat, but fast. I kneel until my skin bruises against the knees, then lay a pillow on the ground and kneel again.

You see I know this girl has not and will never take confession. Nor will she eat of the Blood and Body of the Christ, since at their church they refuse to use *instruments* of Christ, but prefer to use a rock band. Casey has the blood of the Bad Rizal and will never take Communion or confession.

My daughter and her husband come to me more often in the mornings, and also later in the days. I feel them watching me from their doorway, then they come by my chair.

She has her head lowered shamefully, but raises her eyes to me shyly.

Inay, we have something for you, she says.

The husband hands me the picture book, and also a frame he made by his carpenter's hands encasing my portrait of Josephine Bracken. He says the book was on the living room shelf and that there was a misunderstanding. I can feel from the frame that it is made of oak, and the edges carefully sanded. There was a large oak tree in the backyard that his great-grandfather planted, and I know this wood is of that tree.

My daughter steps before her husband, and leans over me. Her eyes look worried and her hands hang folded before her.

13

Why do you cry, Inay? she says.

This husband, his nose has large pores that are red and he tries to touch my daughter's shoulders but she turns away. About his thick neck he wears a shirt that looks to belong to a lumberjack, and I feel sorry for his lack of sense of fashion. My hand nearly reaches out to touch his elbow, to get his attention, but I hesitate, and it is too late.

As the days pass they come to the porch more often, but I do not tell them Casey has the poet's blood. The cornstalks stretch to the sun, and then I watch as my daughter's husband rides over them with a tractor, and they lay snapped and broken like yellow bones among dark clumps of soil.

It snows. After the clouds have gone, the sky does not turn blue again, but remains a silver color. In the distance the trees by the road stand leafless like the ribs of an old broken fan. Sometimes I can see the black buggies of the Amish pulled by trotting horses. My daughter's husband puts a heater on the porch. Still the wind scrapes cold against my cheeks. He sets a pile of blankets at my feet, then lays them over my knees, and wraps them about my body.

My daughter stands watching me, as I pray. I say nothing but she stands there foolishly. Outside I can hear the man who is her husband sawing. The boards of the oak lie carefully shielded from the snow beneath sheets of plastic, and he peels them off in the mornings and saws.

He fashions and affixes a wooden pole to my bathroom walls, handrails that perfectly fit my old palm bones.

It is a help. My body is becoming a burden. With the snow came a pain that lodged in my joints like icicles shaped as knives. The rains followed and with them the close of winter, but still the pains have not gone away. He builds me a crutch so that I may limp out onto my porch, and builds a shorter table so I may eat more comfortably with them in the kitchen. His sister knits me a pillow to sit on, knowing that my legs now easily bruise. They try to get me to eat more, saying I am too thin. They try to get me to take vitamins, though I refuse.

My daughter steps onto the porch while the others are still inside. She hesitates, peering into the lighted house behind her, but then comes

beside me and puts a hand on my shoulder. It is a cold night and I feel
the warmth of her palm through my dress, but I do not say anything
and it lies there unmoving. Finally her fingers stir, and my daughter
asks me about my crying.

She says, Inay, please. We will do anything.

I do not tell her about the blood of Jose Rizal, nor of his mistress. She
will no longer understand.

But she persists, and I tell her about the confession and she bites her
lip and turns away, cupping her elbows. She says nothing, but does not
leave.

They take turns driving me to church; I go four times a week. It is
a long drive, nearly an hour; there are not many Catholics here, you
see. They drive me to the door and help me to my seat, but then the
husband and even my daughter will not stay during Mass. They sit in
their cars instead. My daughter used to go to Mass before dawn for the
nine days in a row preceding Christmas, as we all did. Once I came out
early and found my daughter's husband sitting in the driver's seat with
a Bible open on his lap, his lips mumbling profusely. This was not very
nice to see.

During the Masses I pray for my daughter and for Casey.

I have a plan. When the girl is old enough for confession and first
Communion, I will drive her to the Catholic church. It is an older building, built by German immigrants eighty years ago, and as you approach
its dome and tower poke up above cornfields and reach for the blueness
of sky. She will like it, I think. I have not driven in some time, but for
her I will try. We will have to be careful. My daughter and her husband
must not know.

Their friends from their church come to visit me when I can no longer
walk, and one who works in a hospital brings a wheelchair. It sits large
and angled in the trunk of his big car, the lid popped open, and I know
from its gleaming that it is new and nice. My son-in-law heaves it on his
back and, hunched over, carries it to my porch. I thank them.

They lift me and set me on the wheelchair, and this man wraps a
blanket around my useless legs. I should have been more diligent in car-

15

ing for my legs, I know this now. I will no longer be able to drive Casey to confession. The Catholic church has many concrete steps before it, and although I only fell down a dozen of them, they felt very hard. My daughter's husband ran to where I lay trying to push myself up with my hands, and he picked up my uncooperative body and carried me to the car. The asphalt rushed beneath me like a pebbly stream. Then, as he lay me in the backseat, on vinyl hot against my back even through the cloth of my mourner's dress, he kissed my forehead and called me Grandma. This is the man who will not let my granddaughter make confession. He wiped sweat from his forehead, and took me quickly to his doctor.

Their church friends bring me gifts.

Before meals I hear them and their friends praying in hushed whispers at the table, before sending Casey to fetch me for dinner. Today Casey pushes me in during their prayer unexpectedly, and they prod each other to quietness, and I think from their worried eyes that they have been praying for me, and it spoils my appetite.

After supper, they get their cups of coffee and sit with me on the porch. They pull up folding chairs. They smile more than Catholics do.

The friends say, Grandma, tell us stories about the Philippines.

I tell them out of politeness. But it depresses me to see these people, with their Spartan ways, and to think that my grandchildren will come to this. Already our boys play with their boys, and speak English that is equally rough. It is tiring to talk. And I need my energy to pray.

Three times a week I go to Mass. Now they wheel me into church and set me in back. They even stand behind me, so that they can wheel my chair up for Communion. I believe they talked this over among themselves, and decided it was right to do. They push me past rows of nearly empty pews. I feel the presence of my daughter or her husband behind me, as the Father leans forward to place the host upon my tongue. I wonder if he notices how my daughter does not take Communion. She does not even cross her arms for a blessing. I have not told him who she is. Perhaps he wonders. After the other parishioners have left, I stay and pray some minutes for the girl, and they wait patiently for me to finish.

But they will never let Casey take confession. I know this. My daughter,

I know, believes my worrying is taking a toll on my body, and fears I will die. She pinches my skin with her fingers, to feel how much flesh remains on the bone, like some farm animal, and I tell her to leave me alone. I wish to tell her this will not happen for a long, long time, because first I must make sure about her daughter, although I cannot say this.

Now that I cannot drive, I will have to wait until the girl is sixteen before I can die. When she is sixteen I will have her drive over for confession. Then I can die in peace.

But my daughter and the man who is her husband make it difficult; they do not leave the granddaughter alone with me often. She has chores, and the husband labors now with his carpentry on the grass before my porch, and when he is in the fields or away, my daughter lingers about my wheelchair, trying to feed me cookies and offering me cups of tea and coffee.

I say, Leave me alone.

But she lurks watching behind the screen door, and I feel her shadow.

Before me now, there is a bowl full of uneaten cookies. Also some candies carefully unwrapped. I can smell the corn but also sawdust and I can hear her husband, this man, hammering on some wood to construct an extra bed so that I may lie on the porch. He wipes his forehead with his lumberjack sleeve, and pulls out a saw.

When he hunches over with his saw, it reminds me of Kawayan, when they built my brother's coffin. There was an old acacia tree behind the place where my father's house used to stand, among a yard of tall grass and mango trees, and my brother had men cut the tree into planks to build a new floor for the house of our sister Camille who was going to come back to Kawayan. She had been staying with her son, Bino, in Manila, and planned to stay only until her granddaughter's wedding. But after the ceremony her son would not let her go on. He said there were no doctors on the farm of our youth, but my sister wept and wanted to go. I believe this son thought he was being dutiful, or perhaps feared she would be injured and die and people would talk. But she died soon after of a broken heart, and our brother left those boards on the field, and when he died a year later the peasants of the land who loved him made them into a coffin and laid him into the ground.

I wish to go there someday too, so that I may be buried with my brother and father in the country of Jose Rizal. But I must stay for my granddaughter's sake. She cannot come into my room at night, any longer. My daughter says, Eat Inay, please! and I take the food to my mouth. It is hard, and I have no appetite for food from her hands. But I take it to my mouth for my granddaughter's sake. It is best to be vigilant. She has the blood of Rizal, the eyes of his final mistress.

Old Man

1990s

Late last year my father, a man whom I had not seen in many years, slit his wrists in an unfurnished apartment on the dry dusty foothills of San Diego County. A nurse from the hospital called to inform me that my father was recovering and under suicide watch, and suggested I come over.

He looked so gaunt there, in his hospital bed, his knobby knees visible beneath the thin sheets. He looked so different from the young handsome man I remembered, who'd left us for a mistress and filed for divorce right after running up a credit card debt and filing for bankruptcy. He'd just bought matching BMWs for himself and his girlfriend, an Argentinean dentist whose snooty exiled family lived in Brentwood Park. His wavy Italian hair, his dimples that charmed so many women, the soldier's hardened arms—none of it appeared now on the man before me. His skin had become ashen gray, his hairline receded to show a freckled sallow scalp, his arms turned scrawny, with biceps gone to flab. His eyes seemed larger now, vulnerable in their sockets, as they looked needily up at me.

"Hey Tomas, thanks for showing up," he said. "How'd you know I was here?"

"The nurse called."

"I didn't tell her how to reach you, didn't want to subject you to this," he said.

"I know," I said, not calling him on his lie.

He glanced away, then back again.

"You look good," he said. His smile caused his face to wrinkle, like piecrust that took effort to move.

"Why'd you do it?"

"I'm sorry."

He looked away to stop himself from crying. I worried that I would irritate him and changed the subject. "What you been up to?" I asked. "You living in southern California again?"

"Yeah. For the last two years."

"You didn't like New York?"

"It didn't work out."

"The nurse said you'll be fine. You'll be able to leave here in no time."

"Yeah, they wanted to release me into your care. I refused to let them do that. They just don't want the responsibility."

"What about Catalina?"

"She left me. A year ago."

I nodded. "What have you been up to work-wise?"

"I'm a style consultant."

"No shit."

"Yeah, it's true. Can you believe it?" He reached over to his bedside table and took up a pair of reading glasses from their case. He placed them on his face. They looked expensive with wire rims and a contemporary design, but their youthfulness made his skin look haggard.

"I got these at a discount," he said.

"Do you need anything?"

He hesitated.

"What?"

"Is Gabe around?" he asked.

"No."

"Where does he live?"

"He still lives with Mom. With his girlfriend and daughter in the main house. I live in a bungalow cottage—a shed really—I built out back. So I can pay down her mortgage. We're all together."

My father's face changed. "Gabe didn't want to come here," I said. "But you did."

"I came."

"That's what I meant," he said. "Thanks."

I gave no reply.

"Gabe is the one I'd thought would have come," he said.

"I know it."

He nodded. He pushed his wire-rimmed glasses, which seemed too large for his gaunt formerly handsome face, up on his nose. This made him squint, and I noticed a permanent vertical furrow dividing his forehead. He said, "You'll come back tomorrow?"

On my drive back to Venice, on Los Angeles freeways that bottlenecked near the glistening skyscrapers of downtown, beneath an azure sky windscoured from last night's Pacific Ocean storm, I was thinking about this man I called my father. And I happened to hear an old Neil Young song on the radio, "Old Man." I had loved the melancholy banjo and slide guitar and feeble voice, but never paid attention to the lyrics before. But I caught them now, and the hair stood on the back of my neck.

Hands on the wheel, I froze. Gripped tight. It was that chorus, once repeated, which threw me—like I'd walked into a mirror I hadn't noticed. Yes, maybe I was like him—had that hunger, that need. Images arrested me of my son hugging my leg, tightly pushing his face against my side, saying, "Please don't go, stay and play with me."

"I've got to go, Em. I have to work."

He clung. "Please."

The desperateness of his voice, the wide eyes. That neediness to be loved. On his knees there on the floor, because his hypotonic muscles did not allow him to stand—a genetic ailment that ran down through our extended family, apparently, hitting some of us and not others. Sometimes so mild it went undiagnosed, even unseen. He could read me. He'd see my hesitation, my weakness, and his charming smile came in for the kill, with the lower lip threatening to push out into a cry. And I'd reach down and hug him. I had to go to work, but I'd stay and play his game of Candyland, help finish assembling the Lego castle, push Percy around the Thomas the Train set.

You would not think I was like him by looking at my life, my lonely bungalow, its empty bed, all my nights alone.

But my father. You could look at his life, when I was a kid, and see the old man in the song with that thirsty need. I recalled an image of Dad in bed, wearing his robe, face looking haggard from a bad hangover, yet still young and handsome, as I stood in the door with my backpack.

"Don't go," he said.

"I have school."

"You don't need what those idiot teachers tell you in those stupid books. You think they have something to share with you, some knowledge to pass on that I don't? How many of them have PhDs? Not that my doctorate is good for shit, but you got to wonder about a person like that, why they didn't go for one—a teacher."

"Really, I have to go."

"Don't leave me here. Come on. We'll hit the boardwalk, have some ice cream, walk down to the ocean."

I nervously clutched my bag straps. "I'll get in trouble if I cut class."

"I'll write them a note."

"We've done this too many times already this year. I've hit my limit."

"All right, then. Don't come if you don't want to."

He turned away from me, lips pursed angrily. He faced the wall. He touched his jaw as if someone had punched it with a sledgehammer.

"We can go to the boardwalk after I get out of school," I said. "I'll skip basketball practice."

"Don't bother. I know you don't want to."

"I do want to."

"Maybe Gabe will want to come with me. We'll go fishing."

We ended up going on a deep-sea fishing trip off Marina Del Rey. I was suspended for truancy, but I'd caught ten fish with my father. He taught me how to bait the hooks, reel them in, put the flopping creatures out of their misery by holding them still against the deck in their rucksacks and hammering their heads. He seemed alive now, no sign of his morning funk, his face boyishly smiling, his blue eyes large as Easter eggs, full of contagious spark.

And then, after the divorce, he often came by to take me fishing. He would leave my brother behind. Gabe would sit on the couch with his hands on his lap, muscles tensed, shoulders hunched forward, staring at the carpet, as I got the gear ready and stacked by the front door. Waiting for Dad to arrive. I looked eagerly out the window, at the grainy predawn light, the ghostly outlines of the street. When he pulled up in his black convertible BMW, I gathered up the gear and hurried out the front door so he wouldn't have to come in and rub it in Gabe's face.

You could go for years like this, as a kid, and be thankful for a few days a month or summer. To drink in your time with your father. But I got older and began to see things different, began to unforgive him for what he had done to our mother, how he made her cry, how she couldn't face her extended family for months and avoided the fiestas and barbeques. How we could not even rent movies at the Odyssey since we could not get a credit card, because the man had filed for bankruptcy right before the divorce. How our house took on a mildewy odor because his old fish tanks broke one night, splaying algae-ridden water and baby octopuses and sea urchins and tiny sharks over the blue carpet, along with bright flopping tropical fish—carpet we could not afford to replace. Mom stayed up all night trying to shampoo and scrub the smell away, but gave up near dawn, crying over the orange bucket, and entered a funk she would not get out of again; I latched the door to his old hobby room and plastered the gap along the floor, but the stink still seeped out to the rest of the house. I'd wake up from dreams thinking I could feel the residue of seawater on my skin, which was sticky to the touch.

I stopped returning his calls, and right away he began taking Gabe on our old outings. He took him fishing and camping up in the Sierra. They surfed together. He'd come back smelling of board wax and salt, of kelp that had washed up onshore and warmed in sunlight, sand that he tramped off on our carpet. They went on road trips to Mexico, Santa Fe, a visit to family out in New York. Me, I would not even talk to family on his side. They were all New York Irish and Italians; I spent all my family time with the West Coast Filipinas eating sizzling adobo spooned onto steaming rice, crisp *lumpia*, and empanadas baked with crunchy sugar on their brown crusts.

It outraged me to see my mother's fall. Ika. Her family had once been important in the Philippines. She was related to senators and a president and to Jose Rizal, the great nineteenth-century poet and novelist and beloved national martyr, whose execution by the Spanish led to a revolutionary movement and made him a hero, even the object of a religion. His poems are sung by schoolchildren in that country today. Her mother, Camille, was entered into a contest for Miss Luzon by her patriarch father and became a famed beauty queen whose picture appeared on candy wrappers at age sixteen, to her horror; she tried to escape by running away to a Carmelite convent. The family owns a vast coconut hacienda that was once grand, but now is run-down and without electricity or running water, overrun by jungle and kidnapping Maoists, the family having long ago left for more interesting places—the United States, Europe, Canada, Australia. Nanay Ika herself had been courted by many rich Filipino men. She was a beauty admired for her humble shyness and unusually quiet tongue. She was also addled by an overwhelming capacity for love. In the end, Nanay Ika married this American soldier, my dad, and now my grandmother was routinely taken for a Mexican wetback at the bus stop, we couldn't even get a credit card, and nobody around here has heard of Jose Rizal or could give a fuck about Inay's family name.

On my brother's eighth birthday, Inay threw Gabe a party. She invited all the kids at his school, made the invitation cards herself using parchment paper, colored inks, shapes of cakes and candles cut delicately out of colored tissue paper. She dressed up our house with confetti, bright streamers, hung a piñata in the yard, which she had splurged to buy on Alvarado Street. She bought little gifts for the kids, candies and toys wrapped in small plastic pumpkins. She made the cake herself, yellow with purple *ube* frosting—my brother's favorite, a sweet Filipino root.

The kids were to arrive at noon. Inay hurried about the house making last-minute preparations, fretting because she wanted everything to be perfect for the kids, and because she worried about what the white American mothers would think of our little house, the *ube* frosting, the gift packs, the lunch she'd made. "Nobody likes Filipino food," she fretted.

"You don't know that," I said.

"All our restaurants go out of business," she insisted. "You can find Thai, Chinese, Japanese, Korean everywhere–everything but Filipino!" She wrung her hands and shook her head. "Maybe I shouldn't have made *lumpia* and adobo. Maybe I should have made BLT sandwiches instead."

I reassured her it would be okay.

At ten the doorbell rang. "Someone's early!" my mother panicked.

I set my hand on her shoulder, squeezed it reassuringly, and went to answer it. I opened the door and was shocked to see my father standing there. He wore a tailored black blazer, ink-blue designer jeans, maroon silk shirt, and wing-tip shoes, which I noticed looked expensive. Yet his hair had grown out, and he had a scruffy beard that pressed uncomfortably against his expensive collar, as if it felt confined.

"What are you doing here?"

"Nice to see you too, son," he said. "Can you get Gabe?"

My mother came up behind me. "Russ?"

"I'm here to bring my son to his birthday lunch. I made reservations at the Ivy."

"He can't come," I said.

"It's his birthday. I'm his father. You had him for breakfast and will have him for dinner. It's a Saturday."

"We talked about this, Russ," Inay said. "He's having a party."

"You didn't invite me."

"It's a kids' party."

"Well, I can see I'm not welcome."

"Don't be like this. Please."

He pursed his lips and turned aside, fingering his shirt button as if to keep up his dignity. "Just get Gabe so I can talk to him, wish him a happy birthday."

My mother hesitated, sensing ulterior intentions. She looked at me warily for help.

"He's getting ready," I said. "Why don't you come back later?"

"I live an hour away."

"Dad, you didn't come by last week. You were supposed to take him fishing."

"No, not last week I wasn't."

"Yes you were," I insisted. "He was waiting for you all morning. He sat there on the couch, with his rod assembled and his tackle box at his feet. He refused to eat Mom's eggs, because he said you and him always stopped by McDonald's for breakfast. He didn't eat or put his rod away until two."

"Well, then he got his facts wrong," my father said. "Why didn't he call me? Why didn't you call me?"

"Russ," my mother said.

"He should have called rather than sitting around worrying everybody. Get him here so I can have a talk with him."

"Russ, please." Inay was chewing on her knuckles; she glanced at the front lawn through the window, then at her watch. "The other children and their mothers will soon be here," she said.

He stared at her harshly. "You don't want them to meet me?"

"I don't want Gabe to get upset before the party. You know how long it takes him to recover."

My father nodded as if in agreement. Then he fumbled with his shirt button again, deep in thought, and shook his head. "You're embarrassed of me."

"No, Russ."

"Listen here. You aren't married to me anymore. And I am the boy's father. You have no right to be embarrassed of me. That's not your role anymore. Not your *right*."

He was pacing now, scratching his overgrown beard. It had really gone shaggy, with white ends.

"Dad, why don't you get out of here, please."

He turned on me with a gaze that burned. My cheeks caught fire. He kept his eyes on me for an excruciating moment, then, with the manner of the insulted, he turned down the hall to find Gabe. And I did not go after him. He'd always made demonstrative little gestures when he got drunk and felt Inay was afraid he'd embarrass her; on a trip out to Manila for my cousin's debut, at the Makati Polo Club, he had had too much to drink and tried dancing up her teenage friend, only to stumble over a banquet table and spill punch and liquor over a dozen dresses and white barongs.

I turned to my mother, worried that she'd be crying. But Nanay Ika seemed too busy worrying, glancing back and forth between the front window and then around the room at the party's preparations. The table laid out with festive shimmering purple tablecloth and sparkling gold centerpieces, the colorful streamers hanging from the walls, the yellow HAPPY BIRTHDAY GABE! banner, the balloon clusters pressing up against the ceiling, their strings dangling ready to be taken as a party favor by the little guests.

Against the opposite wall, we'd placed a portable banquet table, covered it in the festive tablecloth, and set dish upon dish of Filipino foods, covered in foil and condensation-beaded cellophane wrap. All cooked for the parents.

To be honest, I felt a little embarrassed that the other mothers would see how much effort Inay put into this, given how few mothers would probably be here. Usually at these parties, several fathers would drop off their kids and disappear to run errands until the ending time. Inay had fretted over this party for weeks, because she knew Gabe was quiet and had few friends. He had seen a speech therapist and there'd been talk of keeping him back a year, and some professional debate among his therapists and teachers over whether he was developmentally delayed or simply exposed to too much Tagalog (Mom's sister, brother, and mother often ate with us and always talked in Taglish). It was decided that the family should try speaking only English. Now, Gabe and I could no longer speak the language, though we could understand it, but less well each year, like memories of old friends and places that fade no matter how hard you try to cling to them by going over them in your mind.

"Look, Tomas, it's Nela and her mother!"

Inay was at the window, but I nudged her to back away so that the approaching pair would not see her looking out.

We waited by the front door for them to knock. She was clenching her elbows tight.

"Relax, Inay. Everything looks great."

"I hope everyone shows up."

"They RSVP'd."

"I know. But there've been so many birthday parties already this fall. Maybe people will change their mind."

"Why don't you open the door?" I suggested.

"Let's let them knock first," she said.

So we waited. "Maybe we should get Gabe," she said. But she made no move to go back there.

"If we go back there now, Dad might come out here and make a scene," I said. "Maybe we should let him say what he wants to say, and then I'll go back and try to get him to go out the back door."

"You think he will?"

"Sure," I said uncertainly.

She looked at me doubtfully, then jumped at the sound of the door knocking. But she put on her best social face and greeted Nela and her mother, a South Asian woman completely Western in clothes and manner, which seemed unusual to me back then. My mother, unlike most Filipinas I know, was not a gregarious person and you could see the effort in her anxious smiles, as she led the girl to the play area she'd set up. She chatted with Nela's mother for a moment, but seemed to struggle with small talk, and glanced at me with pleading eyes, asking me to go back and check on Gabe.

As I went into the hallway, I heard the doorbell ring and the voices of more kids and parents entering.

Our house is rather narrow and long, because the rear was originally a screened porch and you have to access it through a separate hallway closed by two doors. The party voices became muted behind me and I could hear my brother and father talking, as I stood outside Gabe's door. My father sounded unhappy with him, but also a bit eager to please. I knew that tone. It meant that he did not want to be alone.

28

Stiffening, I forced myself to knock. Father's voice hushed, a nee-
dling silence, followed by an irritated "Yes?"

I nudged the door open. They looked at me: Gabe was standing and
my father sat on the edge of my brother's bed.

"We're having a talk, Tomas," Father said.

"Your friends are beginning to arrive," I told my brother.

"We'll be out in a few minutes," our father said.

Gabe was avoiding our eyes, staring at the avocado carpet.

"Actually, if you don't mind using the back exit, I think that would
be best."

"You think that would be best."

"Yeah."

"You're a twelve-year-old boy. Twelve-year-old boys don't talk like
that," he said. He made no move.

"Mom put a lot of effort into this party. You're not going to ruin it," I
said. My voice was trembling. My hands at my sides shook too.

"Fine." He suddenly stood. "Come on, Gabe. We'll go out the back
door. We'll skip this clambake. After the Ivy, we'll head up to Ventura
and do some shore fishing. Get your rod and tackle box."

He started for the back door, and looked back for my brother to follow him. Gabe hesitated. But my brother noticed our father's face begin to crumble, and he went over to his closet and got out his rod and
tackle box.

"Gabe," I said. "What are you doing?"

He avoided my eyes, both of our eyes, as he began to fit the pieces
of his rod together. He was kneeling to screw them tight, keeping his
face away from us, and I thought he was crying. He finished assembling the rod, but stopped there. I thought he was deciding to stay.
We were all quiet. We could all hear the muffled party noise coming
in, the laughing kids and gossiping mothers, even the lower sound
of somebody's father telling some boisterous joke. I had told my
mother to buy a case of fine beer for the parents, and maybe that was
working.

My brother needed a nudge. I approached him to put the rod back in
the closet, got my hand on the pole's thin spry surface. It was an expen-

sive rod our father had bought me several years ago, with money that he was not supposed to have, but I no longer used it. I began to lift it.

"Don't let him take it," my father snapped.

His voice had changed now, to that angry tone, and Gabe held the rod from me. I stopped, then proceeded to peel his fingers off one by one. He did not resist. I took the pole back to the closet, my back turned to our father's face, because I did not want to see his reaction—whether it be anger or hurt.

Then I returned to my brother, who himself was keeping his eyes rigidly focused on his shirtsleeve button as he fingered it; I took his hand and led him toward the inner door, the muted sounds of the waiting party. He tried to look back at our father, but I touched his cheek to redirect his eyes.

My own eyes did, however, catch a glimpse of Father's feet. His polished shoes were awkwardly pigeon-toed, touching at the fronts, nervously tapping, and his hands drooped beneath his knees almost down to his calves as he sat.

I expected him to call out to us, or even to set his hand on my back. But he did not. However, as we left the room I could hear his heavy breathing.

We did not look back, as we made our way to Gabe's party: I held my brother's elbow, and pulled him against me tight.

The Last Participant

I

Bong's family emigrated from the Philippines through London, where they lived with a distant aunt in a neighborhood filled with Indians and Pakistanis and immigrants from the East Caribbean. The children from the council buildings played in the multistoried stairwells and on the nearby streets. The white kids thought he was Indian, and one girl asked him if his mother pissed while standing on the toilet seat. When she discovered that he came from a former U.S. colony, she grew interested, as did the other kids, and she made him tell a group of Indians that the *yanks* had had a colony too. They thought it was funny that he seemed proud that he'd had a better colonizer than they had, in his opinion. Someone read a newspaper article about a Manila garbage pile in which thousands of Filipinos lived, and about rural families so poor they would send a daughter to become a Manila prostitute so the siblings could eat and go to Catholic school. He lied and told them all this was untrue, and got a cornea scratched in a fight. Six months later his family moved on to Los Angeles—Bong was at the age of thirteen—and he was shocked to discover that none of the students here seemed to know what a Filipino was.

"Your name is *what?*"

"Bong Bong."

THE LAST MISTRESS OF JOSE RIZAL

"What kind of a name is Bong Bong?"

"Filipino."

"What the fuck is a Filipino?"

Bong smiled his tight ingratiating smile. "Oh nothing," he said cheerfully, with a dismissive wave. "Just a little country in Asia."

A little country where over half a hundred million people thought they were Americanized, where English was an official language, where he had been taught to memorize and recite the Gettysburg Address at school, where a bunch of people aspired to become more like the *Amerikanos* and believed they had a special relationship—a friendship—with the *Amerikanos* owing to their common history. He was so ashamed he never brought up the issue again.

He changed his name. That felt better. Bong Bong was only a nickname anyway, and he started using his given one, Rafaelito. He figured he would keep it until he went back to the old country, after college. However, sixteen years later he still lived in Los Angeles (his parents never returned to Manila), and the new name no longer seemed strange to him.

II

He followed them from a distance. She lived in an apartment complex only three blocks away, and because the boyfriend was a scriptwriter and producer who had no steady hours, they walked her dogs by his apartment almost daily on their way down to the café on Wilshire Boulevard, just as she and Rafaelito used to do. Their route took them right by his window. He tried not to look outside at this time. Yet because the dogs wanted to relieve themselves according to a routine, the couple passed at almost the same moment each morning, and Rafaelito needed only to linger near the window at about 9:45 a.m. and he would see them passing, his aching eyes squinting at the sunny sidewalks. She liked to wear tight black yoga pants—which left visible her silky calves—large Italian sunglasses, and fine leather sandals; she always held the tall man's hand like a clinging teenager, and gripped the three dog leashes in the other. The three beasts (a German shepherd and two Akitas) tugging her forward as if she were a light balloon. The man wore shorts and sandals and a pricey black Patagonia rock climber's jacket; his legs were the color of sweet bourbon.

When she dumped him she had said, "I'm just so tired Rafaelito."

"Are you saying you don't believe in me?"

"No, of course I believe in you. I've always said so. And I know you're going to make it on your own someday. Someday soon."

"So then why are you dumping me?"

"Oh, honey. I'm not dumping you. I'm just tired. We need a break. We'll get back together, probably, I'm sure. But I'm just tired and need a little rest. I do believe in you, but you don't believe in yourself and it gets exasperating sometimes."

He looked at her bags: a Tumi overnight toiletry case, and three plastic grocery bags she had filled with books and jazz CDs and random pieces of clothing, her incense packets whose scent filled his home. The fact that he had done so well in academics, and had excelled on a full scholarship at a private eastern college, made him feel all the more like a failure in everything else.

"I know you'll find somebody else," he said. "A woman like you, attractive, young, could get a guy who's already made it."

"That's not very nice, Rafaelito."

"I'm sorry."

She sighed. "Okay."

"Well, so when are you going to come back?"

"Rafaelito, I can't think about that now. I need to breathe. I need to take my stuff and go."

A week passed, two weeks passed, and yet she did not come back as she suggested she would. ("That's not correct, Rafaelito. I never promised anything." "You said you would come back. You explicitly said that, and when you say something it might not have been an explicit promise, but you've given your word." "How is that giving my word, Rafaelito? I don't think so." "You have said, in words, that you would come back to me, that you just needed a little time alone, a breather, you were tired, then you would come back." "No, I don't think that's the meaning of giving your word. You're taking advantage of my not having a fancy Vassar education. Just because I went to Moorhead State.")

A week later he saw her in a movie theater line at the indoor mall with another man, waiting to see a foreign feature. He stopped. His breath caught inside him. Even out in the mall, he could smell buttery popcorn emitted from the theater doors. His throat felt greasy. They were not holding hands and it was possible that he was only a friend, but Rafaelito noticed that it was a French film and that the poster gave an impression of a sexy feature. Far above him, the mall ceiling was a great arch of tinted glass, beyond which drifted the underbellies of sunny clouds: their faint shadows moved across the mall floor as he decided to buy a ticket and follow them in. He worried he wouldn't find them, but saw them in the concession line. He observed the man's long taut neck, the tanned Adam's apple, but he could not make out who paid for the food. He sat in back but could not discern them in the dark, where his sagging seat smelled of urine. The movie that unfolded before him began as something enchanted and magical, full of bright colors of clothes and umbrellas that moved over the backdrop of a gray, World War II–era French town. It was about a beautiful French girl who falls in love with a boy—also a virgin, and equally unsullied by the emotional residue of past lovers, equally innocent. She finally sleeps with him the night before he departs for the German front. At first the love story was wondrous, full of Technicolor and singing, something innocent. Rafaelito thought: now that was a different time, when people were loyal, constant, and saved themselves. Then her belly grew. The boy was away at war, no letters, her mother worried townspeople would begin to notice. She married another man who loved her so much he would raise her boy as his own, while the boy was still cut off at the front and had only known her. He returned to find her. Rafaelito gripped his seat arm, winced, and turned away.

At the end, when the soldier boy—now years later and a man—saw her at a gas station with the child who was his son, Rafaelito wept like a mute baby in the theater dark.

He went out into the mall, blinking under skylights, startled by the flood of daylight. He waited at a safe distance for them to emerge. But they must have taken a different exit because he did not see them departing into the sparse shopping crowd.

III

She had liked his kid brother, Nino, from the first time she saw them together in Douglas Park running like children over the drained concrete basin where water sprayed up from the ground in shimmering spurts like man-made geysers, then fell back down on them like cool rain. He noticed her watching him, while a little redheaded girl played at her knees. Then he forgot about her and sometime later Nino fell and splayed his knee. Rafaelito made his brother sit on a concrete bench, and washed the wound where the skin had slid away. He pulled off his own wet shirt and soaked it in hope of making it clean, then knelt down to wrap it over Nino's knee. However, a shadow came over the ground and a feminine voice asked him if he needed a bandage. She was standing over him, smiling, offering a bandage from a plastic automobile first aid kit she had obviously bothered to retrieve from her car. He thanked her and took it and wrapped Nino's leg. After he finished, he explained that they did not normally run through the park's waterspout but today it was so hot.

"You don't have to apologize to me," she said. "I don't own the park."

"I know, but you've got a kid and I don't. I don't think I'm supposed to be here without one."

She looked over Nino more carefully. Rafaelito's shy brother must have seemed younger than twenty-two to her—he was small and held himself bashfully and had beautiful skin as yet unblemished by sun or acne. He looked down and Rafaelito noticed that his brother's hands trembled like his own.

He took her to a movie, surprised that she agreed to let him—he'd taken the chance in asking her only because she was new to LA and admitted being homesick for Minnesota, and feeling out of place. She

35

looked intimidated by all the people they passed in the lobby, the girls in skinny black and the men in actual stylish clothes, and he managed not to shove his hands in his pockets as they walked.

Afterward she agreed to let him buy her a drink, and he took her to the bar at the Bel Air Hotel, which didn't charge a cover fee, and they talked in the warm fireplace light beside the piano.

The girl at her knees had been her niece, visiting from Minnesota, who had already returned home. She missed her. She fingered her straw, clinking ice, stirring her green drink. Then she smiled and said she liked his brother whom she had thought was only a child as he ran through the glistening fountain rain. She said it was sweet that they played together, and nice that Rafaelito looked after him for his parents.

He told her he did not take care of him. Nino was twenty-two.

"Twenty-two?"

"He looks younger than his age."

"But I thought he was a *kid*. Even when I got a closer look at him, I still thought he was no more than fourteen."

"He's a bit bashful. And a bit small. A childhood sickness."

"What sickness?"

Rafaelito waved his hand and tried not to blush. "Nothing serious. Just tuberculosis."

She looked as though she felt sorry for his brother, and on the way back to the car she took his hand. She seemed to notice that he didn't like to talk about his brother's sickness; he didn't tell her the reason—that he worried he'd been at fault for hogging up his brother's portions at meals when they were poor and Nino should have still been growing, leaving the boy weak and susceptible.

He showed her the city as if he were a native, and she seemed to believe that he possessed a great amount of knowledge about the metropolis, though in truth he did not—you could never really know such a big place. He took her to the hill on Griffith Park, where they could sit on the cool grass and look over the glistering metropolis basin at night; to Cantor's on Fairfax for face-steaming matzo ball soup at 2:00 a.m.; and over the curving roads of Bel Air to find Reagan's house. He showed her Raymond Chandler's old Hollywood Hills home that was said to be haunted and then the restaurant at Paradise Cove where they sipped sweet cocktails on the sand surrounded by purple Malibu Mountains that jutted out on either side of the bay.

They made love outside, beneath a blanket on the cool sand, peering out to make certain strangers were not approaching them in the darkness, her muted cries humbled by the rumbling of invisible waves.

"Isn't Nino lonely?" she said over breakfast at the Rose Café. She fingered his hand beneath the table, leaning forward to be heard among the restaurant clatter.

"What makes you say that?"

"I've been hogging up your time."

"That's okay."

"He doesn't seem like he makes friends easily."

"Well, no. That's true."

"Does he have friends at work?"

"He doesn't really work. He reads scripts for money, at home, while he tries to write them. Like everyone else around here," Rafaelito added with a dismissive wave of his hand.

"That's no way to meet people."

"I know."

"You don't need to act embarrassed of your brother just because he writes scripts," she said.

Her face had changed in a way he had not seen before. He heard a light thumping and realized that his knee was trembling against the table leg.

"Actually, he's good at doing scripts," Rafaelito said. "It's just that we write them together. I guess what I'm saying is that I'm not being embarrassed *of* him. I'm being embarrassed for myself."

The hard look on her face that had made his legs shake beneath the table softened now into a smile, and she reached under the tabletop and laid her hand on his knee.

IV

He tried not to think about her. It was pathetic, but he couldn't stop. He could not help thinking about the time his father first met her—the stunned look on his face at the sight of her, the blue eyes that seemed to take up half her face, and the skin that looked purer than the inside of a conch shell, the face that rose above Daddy's head—the man must have been thinking about how much lovelier she looked than those stuck-up Mestizo families with their pidgin Manila Spanish with its fake Castilian accent and the haughty *bayot* houseboy at the Polo Club who had sent him around back with his package, right in front of his son, with a stick up his ass just because he worked for Mr. D from San Francisco, California. How his mother's hand trembled as she stirred the broth for dinner, wanting it to be perfect. It was her idea of an American dish, filled with cut up hot dog and Spam one could smell in the steaming pinkened rice. Jennifer smiled and pretended to like it. His father took them on an overnight deep-sea fishing trip, one that must have cost him a fortune, and later cooked the catch for a crowded dinner—and Rafaelito cringed when he realized the man had invited their relatives to show off his son's girlfriend.

She wandered off from the loud gregariousness of the kitchen to his brother's bedroom (Nino still lived with his parents in the tiny room the brothers once shared) to use the bathroom, then lingered by the bookshelves to examine Rafaelito's old yearbook. A film script lay nearby, held together by three brass Chicago screws and she read it. When Rafaelito found her there, sitting cross-legged with her back against the bed, she was on page twenty and already crying. It bore both brothers' names, but Rafaelito did not yet tell her that Nino had basically written it himself.

V

He knocked on the coarse surface of her front door, its brown stain dried from the sun, splintered and faded. After a moment he heard her light footsteps approaching on the clicking tiles and then a hesitation.

The light went out within the eyehole, then another full minute passed before the door partially opened and she peered out at him.

"What are *you* doing here?"

He managed to convince her to let him inside, and they sat in the familiar living room on opposite chairs of cool sinking leather.

"Listen, I'm about to make it," he said. "Didn't you know? I've been talking to Dream Factory about a movie. They like my ideas. My agent showed them my Hatfield and McCoy script. People around town have been loving it. She says that my days of being overlooked are over. I'm talked about now, *known* around town for my dialogue and 'tender' portrayals of family conflict."

"You sold the Appalachian script? That's great."

"Well, no. People are afraid to make the feud film because it's too literary, too dark, and it doesn't have a happy enough ending. But this one production company loved it so much and wanted to work with me so much that they came up with an idea for me to work on, a more commercial one, an alien invasion movie. I know that sounds hokey but it actually has some similar themes to do with family relations and such, similar to the Appalachia manuscript."

"You're doing an alien invasion movie with your brother?"

"No, the company only wanted me. They didn't want to have to deal with too many people."

She swept a strand of disheveled hair from her face, and her brow furrowed as she tucked it behind an ear. "But I thought Nino wrote the Appalachian script," she said.

"Well, he mostly did. Sure. But that was just a writing sample, and only one of several which I wrote and put his name on too."

"Like the one where the White House dog is kidnapped. You wrote that one, right?"

"Yeah, okay, I know you didn't like that one. But I also did a lot of work on the Appalachian manuscript. I came up with the concept and I streamlined the story. You should have seen what a mess the first draft was. I basically script-doctored a messy novel into another medium, one that requires tighter plotlines and structure, and that's what most interested Dream Factory."

"I thought that White House dog movie was sort of *derivative*."

"Yeah, well we're not talking about that one now."

She shook her head. "I can't believe you're doing this to Nino."

"I'm not doing anything to Nino."

"Yes you are."

"Listen, I don't think I'm making myself clear. Nino knows about the Dream Factory thing. He wouldn't be interested in working on an alien invasion movie."

"He's poor. He lives with your *parents*. He could use the money."

"But you didn't see the face he made when I told him about Dream Factory's interest. If those producers had gotten a sense of how much he despises them, it would've ruined the whole project. Listen. I'm going to have Nino help me, and I'll pay him. The Dream Factory people just don't want to have to deal with so many credited players officially on the project. And, like I said, Nino agreed."

"Of course he's going to agree with what you said, Rafaelito. He's so timid and does whatever you tell him to. You've got some sort of a weird power going on with him. I think it's a bit creepy, to tell you the truth. I mean, you've been nice to me, almost timid and deferential, actually, but it's like you have to be the opposite with your brother. If all this is your attempt to make me want to change my mind and go back to you, it's actually having the opposite effect."

"Change your mind? I thought you'd said you *were* coming back."

"You're reminding me of how pissed off I get whenever I see you stepping all over your sweet brother," she said. "And this derivative pseudo-Hollywoodish way you're talking, it's like you don't know who you really are, can't really be yourself."

Rafaelito flushed. He did not mention his recollection of her stepping all over himself; nor did he remind her, in the face of her new artistic snobbishness, how she had formerly accused him of being too "idealistic" and "impractical" and how at this rate he was going to be poor forever, and while that was all noble and admirable and whatnot, she was getting worried, tired of eating in all the time and having to turn down nights out with friends to save money, not to mention her biological clock and the necessity to feed and clothe and house a child someday.

Instead, he folded his hands deferentially before him, like some meek penitent, in a manner that he knew disgusted her, and began pleading with her to let him back in.

As he spoke she was sitting on a red leather couch they had once made love on, stained with the dried liquid of their intermingled sex, on which she had held and comforted him and sat on his lap and kissed his eyelids, but now she had her pretty legs tightly crossed beneath a blue satin robe with lace fringes he had never seen before, hard-sole sandals, her arms crossed as she stared at him severely.

He said, "I promise you, Nino is fine with the Dream Factory thing. In fact, he tells me almost daily how grateful he is that I pushed him into writing screenplays in the first place. It's his calling. Nothing else worked for him. And I do have a lot of plans for him. And this way he's got time freed up to work on an independent type of feature, which he's going to direct and I'm going to produce."

"Nino direct."

"Sure."

"Directing requires ordering people around," she said. She looked aside, in the direction of the kitchen, which had new Tuscan-style curtains up, and shook her head.

"Nino is fine with people when he has a purpose for dealing with them. Okay, he's bad at parties and nebulous social events, small talk, et cetera. But in the service of making his vision, his *dream*, he can deal with them fine. In fact, many of the best directors are shy, introverted-type people."

Jennifer looked at him severely. "You should leave him alone, Rafaelito."

"So, are you coming back yet or what? Because I'm getting sort of tired of waiting. I'm getting, to be frank, a little lonely. It seems that we've had a reasonable amount of breathing time now."

Rafaelito watched with alarm as her expression grew increasingly incredulous. He felt his heart in his throat. He recalled the scene in *Annie Hall* where Woody Allen flew all the way over to Los Angeles to try to win Diane Keaton back, and ordered a sandwich with alfalfa sprouts at an outdoor café under glaring overexposed light. "And I was thinking, maybe we should get married," he said.

41

"Oh, Rafaelito. You're kidding me."

"Well, no."

"But this is so, so out of the blue."

"Well, you've talked about your biological clock, wanting to have kids. We talked about a future together. And we've got all this history behind us."

"Oh Raffy."

At least she was giving him this. Yet he also feared he was frightening her. "Okay, look," he said. "I didn't mean to spook you. It was just a thought, an idea to think over. No pressure, right?"

She regarded him in an odd, puzzled manner, and this time he looked away.

That afternoon he walked down the avenue. Now the slender girls often pushed strollers, designer and foreign, and they had thin hips that did not look as if they had ever parted to birth a child. He peered in at the babies, trying to appear unsuspicious; he noticed their cute hats and red cheeks and fat smiles and colorful pacifiers that bobbed on their mouths like perched butterflies. He imagined these young mothers with their husbands. He felt sick with longing, the way he imagined only women did, a maternal instinct, and sat at an outdoor restaurant table and rested until a worker came outside and told him he had to order something or go away.

VI

He entered the café and saw them sitting at a corner table. He ducked outside and watched through the tinted window as they read their *New York Times*, and sipped on iced lattes, and when the boyfriend left for the bathroom Rafaelito hurried over and walked up to her.

Her face, which smiled as she read some human interest newspaper story, changed as she looked up at him.

"Hi," he said.

She just stared at him.

"I was walking around and I saw you."

"Have you been following me?"

"Following you? What kind of an accusation is that? I live up the street, remember?"

She studied him and her face softened. "Sorry."

"That's okay," he said.

A silence.

She tapped her burgundy fingernails on the table. "Well, how have you been?"

"Fine," he said. He spoke sulkily, but noted irritation in her expression and tried to modify his tone. "Actually, things have been going well," he added cheerfully.

"Good. Good."

"Yeah, the Dream Factory thing is happening. I've actually received an actual check. Can you believe it?"

"Great, wow. I always told you I believed in you more than you believed in yourself."

"And so, well, how *are* you?" he asked, then before she could speak added, "Can I sit down? I mean, I'm interested in hearing about how you've been."

She glanced toward the restrooms. "Well, my boyfriend is here. He's in the bathroom."

A silence passed.

"But, okay, if you want to rest up for a minute," she said.

He sat.

He asked her about her life and she obliged. Her boyfriend was the gist of the story. She spoke as if Rafaelito were an old girlfriend, or gay friend, or Harmless Asian Male Friend, and left out no details apart from the most pornographic. They were in love. They liked to hike and bike together and had already gone on several vacations, once to Maui, once to Napa, once to Telluride. Brandon—("That's his name, just like your brother-in-law, can you imagine that?")—had a condo in Hawaii just across from the Kapalua Ritz Carton. He bought it when on a shoot there and fell in love with the island, even though buying was so impractical when you could just stay at hotels for less.

"What was he filming?" Rafaelito asked.

She paused. "Oh just a dumb comedy thing. He mostly does TV."

"Well, it pays the bills."

"Actually he was a dramatist before, Off-Off-Broadway, even got a Guggenheim. But his playwright friends were all moving to Santa Monica, doing sitcoms and getting their houses profiled in *Architectural Digest*, and begging him to come out here and keep them company among the Philistines" (Jennifer laughed, apparently enjoying a personal joke). "He's doing a play at the Westwood Playhouse, though. He calls stage work his 'hobby'—you know, like William Faulkner did."

Rafaelito felt very low and sulky. He was sweating even though this room was air-conditioned like an igloo, and frosty fake air rippled his T-shirt like a breeze off an iceberg entering through an Inuit's open doorway. At this point two months ago, she would have looked at him sympathetically and touched his knuckles, looking into his eyes maternally, with her own huge blue irises, which had made grown men fall into deep merciless puppy love, and asked what was the matter.

However, she now appeared to be remembering something about Rafaelito she did not like, and he sat more upright.

"So where's this Brandon guy from?" he said.

She stared at him. "You know, I think this conversation was a mistake. I think maybe it needs to end."

"What? What did I say? All I did was ask about your boyfriend? I was being polite."

"Yeah, polite."

"Hey look, don't make out like I'm the one being rude here."

"Fine. I don't care. Can you please go now, before Brandy gets back?"

"Brandy? Is that your nickname for him?"

"And how is that any of your business?"

"Because you got it from me."

"I don't think so."

"That's what my sister calls her husband, Brandon."

"I didn't name my boyfriend after your brother-in-law. Jesus, Rafaelito, I didn't realize you were *that* narcissistic."

"No, what I mean is: how many grown men named Brandon call

themselves Brandy? None. I've always called Brandon Brandy behind his back, and you must have picked up on that and use it now on your boyfriend."

"Meaning?"

"Meaning we should get back together. It proves that even with this guy you're thinking of me, at least subconsciously."

She looked at the ceiling, paused, and then looked back at him again. "I don't think about you, Rafaelito."

"You don't have to lie, out of misguided loyalty to him. I mean, you've only been with for him for what, a month or two? Whereas we have all that history behind us. All the memories, and experiences together. Don't you see? It's inevitable, natural that your subsequent relationships will bear the lingering influence of ours. We're a part of each other, inextricably bound."

"I never heard you call your brother-in-law Brandy."

"Sure you did."

"No, I don't think so."

"Look. I remember clearly, it was a running joke between us. You were so mad about the way he treated me, you said he looked down on me and didn't take me seriously and you were even angry with me for not standing up for myself, and so you mocked him too. Like that time at my parents' house over Christmas last year? Anyway we had a laughing fit in their backyard. Like we had after you met Tessy and heard her call him Brandy for the first time. All this happened between us."

Rafaelito waited for her reaction.

"You need to leave now."

"What?"

"Look, you obviously have a lot of memories, real or imagined, about us which I don't have. You obviously sit around thinking about it too much. It's over. You need to get a life. I'm through talking to you now."

"Now listen here, we had a long time together, and you hurt me."

His voice had wavered. She did not reach out to set a slender knuckle against his cheek.

"Well, maybe I did hurt you. You say I did so I'll have to grant you that. Maybe you made more of our relationship than I did, or than you

45

were meant to. I don't know. I'm sorry. But I know that I did you a favor by cutting you off from what was, essentially, an unhealthy, unequal relationship. I mean, you obviously were spending more time thinking about me than I was about you, you were more invested in our relationship emotionally, and you were even, well, I'll say it: submissive. I don't know what kind of scars you had from past relationships, but you learned a way of relating which you foisted onto me. It's obvious you think I've been a bitch to you, but I am not like that with other people. I know I'm actually a nice person, a good person. People say that about me. I'm *known* as a sweet person, a role model, and an *example*, actually, known for my values. So I can't have been a bad person to you, unless you were encouraging that kind of a dynamic. Well, so I unwillingly had some sort of power over you. This much I can understand looking at you now, even though I can barely remember what happened so briefly between us."

She tugged her little purse up on her shoulder, pulling the strap tight, and added, "So I cut you loose and now you're free to find someone who isn't going to be so 'neglectful' of your feelings, to use one of your own favorite words. You're on your own now. You're responsible for yourself. My hands are clean of you."

"This isn't fair, Jennifer. You scarred me deeply."

"You let yourself be scarred. If you were healthy and confident it wouldn't have happened. You shouldn't have taken our relationship so deeply. The fact is, *I was never impacted on a very deep level by our experience*, so I don't see why I should have to think about it now."

"The reasoning there doesn't make sense, honey."

She stood, enraged.

"You get the fuck out of here, do you hear me? I don't remember you. We never had a relationship together. We were friends with privileges, and those privileges are gone, and now so is the friendship too. It never happened. I don't remember you, so it never happened. I never wronged you, I never changed you. And if you approach me I will not acknowledge your existence."

"Jesus, Jennifer. Will you keep your voice down? What's the matter with you?"

At this point he sensed the man approaching. The man was taller and more athletic looking than Rafaelito had realized, his chin more chiseled, his swimmer's legs more long and tan and golden and beautiful, and all the casualness had left his now tense body.

"What's going on here, Jennifer?" he said. The man stared hard at Rafaelito.

"I don't know. This guy came in through the door and just started talking to me as if he knew me. I told him to leave me alone, and he won't stop."

"Jennifer, what are you talking about? How can you say all this?"

"Listen, Buddy. You need to leave my fiancée alone. You need to get out of these premises. *Now.*"

"Look, this is weird. She's not being straight, I don't know why. The fact is, she's my ex-girlfriend. We went out together for two years. She must've told you about me. Rafaelito Bautista."

He shook his head.

"She never mentioned me?"

"Nope."

"But she went on a fishing trip with my dad, and came over for dinner with my family one Christmas."

The man shook his head.

"Who'd she tell you she went with before she met you?"

"Not Rafaelito Bautista," the man said as he took a hold of Rafaelito's shirt and hauled him toward the glass doors with the help of a young Filipino employee with an amiable goatee and firm hands; the boyish fellow had a newcomer's thick Manila accent. A crowd of patrons was watching him helplessly getting tugged out, including many faces familiar from his walking here daily over the course of three years, among them an elegant middle-aged woman he'd spoken to about her son at Penn, a woman who apparently did not remember their conversation or that he had been with Jennifer then, as this lady disgustedly shook her head at Rafaelito now.

The sidewalk glared beneath him as his buttocks fell down on it, slamming hard against his tailbone. He fell back, his palms ripped on the grainy concrete, and he tasted the grimy curb on his tongue.

"Jesus, that was so unnecessary. You hurt me."

"Don't you ever come in here again," the Filipino barista said.

Rafaelito had had several conversations with him, had even spoken Tagalog to the friendly man, but in his eyes there was no recognition and only coldness now.

But I shared your bed, you stroked my face, I made you feel deeply enough for you to say I love you, we made coffee together, you walked my dogs who miss you and would recognize your scent, you swallowed my seed, we touched tongues and traded saliva—and did you know that our mouths carry bacteria that are permanently implanted by all those whom we have kissed? We made common memories which live in us, or at least me, are you saying you have wiped that history clean?

He was disgusted with himself for having these thoughts. He wished he could forget them and forget himself. He wanted to be like her. He wanted to be like her boyfriend. He was sick of himself and he hated himself and he was gripped by a sudden urge to go to his mother's home and confess his baseness and seek her forgiveness and love.

VII

As he limped back toward his apartment, each right step forward caused his tailbone to push into a mushy developing bruise, so he tried to keep the weight on his other leg. He had to drag himself past the park, and mothers at the sandbox looked at him warily as if being an apparent cripple meant he were a predator, or perhaps it was something in his face; he looked down. Mama used to bring him here and Nino and Tessy would hunt with him in the pond for baby frogs; back then he had gotten all the compliments, over his chubby cheeks and oversized smile, and even into his twenties he had been told he had a trustworthy face. He had believed then that a boyishly trustworthy face was repugnant to young women, and tried to rid himself of it, and apparently he had succeeded.

The street here had only tall, thin useless palm trees for shade, and by the time he limped to his apartment he was sweating and sunburned;

his eyes stung from glare. His tongue throbbed and swelled from where he bit it as he swore at himself for his stupid words.

A relationship with only one participant left, he thought. How pathetic.

He tried not to cry or feel sorry for himself, but at some point he passed the hallway mirror and noticed his own image and froze, stunned at the sight of the swollen-eyed miserable wreck of an ugly person he saw there. He no longer looked young, no longer had the boyishness that had seemed to curse him into not being taken seriously at work or by women, the child's face that Mama had loved and Jennifer had claimed to too; his flesh was sour and haggard from all the dry air and repressed bitterness and habitual worry, and his shoulders slouched forward.

He tried to smile, but the sallow cheeks sagged, the laugh lines crinkled like piecrust, and he had to turn away.

It was not the face he thought of as his own. It was not the sort of face that would draw other people to want to know him, he knew, because it would not have drawn even himself, if it had belonged to a stranger.

For Lunch at a Filipino Restaurant We Go to Koreatown

I

Jennifer once took him to her Lutheran Church for a Young Adults Group meeting. They met in a church hall, and he had been surprised at how attractive and hip-looking everyone seemed; the food laid out on a nice banquet table was Scandinavian ("Norwegian," she explained to him. "Back in Minnesota all the Lutheran Churches each have their own ethnic affiliations and foods–Norwegian, Swedish, German. We're funny that way."). He was amazed at how much food there was, and how beautifully it had been laid out, on real dishes, and at how much time people had put into cooking and presenting it. At his own church, the nuns had laid out chips and store-bought donuts on paper plates at flimsy foldable tables, and they had donation baskets with suggested prices on them written in felt marker, like at a garage sale. ("Here, try this," she said and gave him a dessert plate with a slice of lingonberry pie on it. Everyone was amazed that he had never tasted the fruit before.)

Later–much later–she asked him to take her to a Filipino restaurant. They had been arguing again, and it seemed like a strange request. He told her he only knew of one, and it was a long drive away. Maybe it would be better to go to his mother's home–she would be happy to make them some *kaldereta* and sizzling *sisig*. Jennifer said,

50

"No, *I want to go to the restaurant.*" He shrugged and complied. They drove on the freeway through forty minutes of traffic. He got off in a neighborhood in which she locked her passenger door and tried not to look anxious as she watched the passing bungalows with barred windows, dilapidated liquor stores, and cheap gospel churches, and then the neighborhood seemed to get better and the stores at least had no graffiti or Mexican signs, and she realized that the signs were an Asian language.

"What language is all that?" she said excitedly. "Is that yours?"

"No. I don't know what it is. Korean or something."

"There's so much of it."

He shrugged.

They passed billboards with smiling Korean faces advertising expensive things. They passed stores with signs in Korean with fancy electronics and hip, upscale salons and clean-looking restaurants.

"It's so nice here," she said. "Affluent."

"Yes it is."

He had taken his mother here once, and she had looked at all this sadly. She said she hadn't realized how well the Koreans were doing, just like the Japanese, and look how many of them there were. All these upscale stores, going on for miles. Once she had dreamed of starting a restaurant with her brother to sell her *lechon* and *leche* flan and *biko* and adobo that American friends like, but that had never come to anything. "Just a bunch of dreamers," his mother said. She tapped her cigarette ash out the window, then added, "My father chained himself with some other old veterans to the city hall, demanding some army benefits or something that Roosevelt had promised them. Your grandfather's friend called the TV station and a woman there said they would film the protest. The old men got excited and wrote out signs in markers and dressed in suits and invited their friends and wives to come and watch. They chained themselves to something on the city hall steps, and everyone waited for the TV van. But no TV people showed up. At home I watched the channel and looked for Papa, but they covered a high school spelling bee instead. I did not tell your grandfather. That night he came home with a cheerful smile and ate three servings of my food. But later I heard through his bedroom door the muffled sounds of his crying. He never mentioned the war to the family again."

Rafaelito had secretly called the station to ask why no vans had been sent to film his grandfather. The secretary said to wait and a few minutes later a woman came on. She sounded nice. She said that they had intended to go, until they found out that these protests had already been covered. Apparently they happened last year, and many times before. A van had been sent then, she said happily.

II

Rafaelito never told his mother that there had been one more time, actually, when the old man did speak of the war. He'd found Lolo drunk one evening, in the alleyway behind the apartment, like some vagrant in the bushes. Rafaelito noticed a bottle of gin in his hand, almost empty, but when he tried to take it out of the old man's hand, Lolo woke, eyes wide with outrage, and pulled the bottle closer to his chest.

"It's just me, Lolo—Rafaelito."

"Get away from me you rich man's bastard. *Anak sa labas!* Or I will beat you with this glass!"

"What are you talking about?"

"You think you are better than me because you have the blood of the former president? He was a puppet of the Japanese! That is like a Frenchman bragging about being related to the president of Vichy France!"

"Lolo, you're talking nonsense," he said and took the bottle roughly now out of his *lolo's* hands, the fingers slippery against the glass as he pried them off. This time the old man let him, but he looked at Rafaelito strangely, without love or affection, and Rafaelito felt his ears burning.

"Nonsense? You would have me believe you don't know the rumors?"

"Please, Lolo. Let's go inside."

"*Ay Dios ko*, are you are *crying*? Yes. You must know."

He took Lolo's old soft hand and began to lead him to the backyard and up the old wood steps, slowly, one weathered board at a time. The boards wobbled, creaked, peeling paint crunched beneath his feet.

They had to pause near the top, for the old man to lean on him and rest, and then he felt the man's finger touch his face, trying to dry it. "I'm sorry, Grandson. You really didn't know."

"Didn't know what?"

"Why do you think we left Kawayan Hacienda so suddenly and fled the country? *Ay*, your *nanay* was already married but just a little girl. It wasn't the *haciendero* who did it, but a son. Your papa was so humiliated, he has never gone back, even when his *nanay* died and the funeral was in Manila. He could have left your mother, but didn't. He never saw his own *nanay* again."

III

Rafaelito had Jennifer direct him with a map and they found the strip mall, full of posh Korean stores and a lone Filipino restaurant. Inside it was decorated with heavily lacquered bamboo and cheesy fake thatch. Pots were filled with plastic orchids, which Jennifer touched to make certain they truly were not real. Rafaelito nervously shoved his hands in his pockets as she fingered a cardboard box whose cut-open front displayed a nativity set, decorated with large-bulb Christmas lights—though it was July. There were many tables on the red industrial carpet, giving the place the feel of a cheap convention center, but the tables were all empty.

They sat quietly. She looked out the window at some young Koreans in fashionable designer clothes. One girl wore a silky white quilted jacket, her furry collar embracing her lovely neck and cheeks.

"Well, are you glad you came here?" he asked. His pulse rose in his fingertips that lay on the warm smudged-glass tabletop, which protected the embroidered tablecloth.

"Sure."

"Good."

She said, "Why is this place in Koreatown?"

53

"I don't know."

"But where's the Filipino town?"

He shrugged. "I don't think there is any."

"None? Why not?"

He waved his hand and laughed nervously. "We all want to avoid the gossips."

She did not laugh.

"Anyway, I suppose there aren't enough of us."

"No, I read there are more of you than them," she said. "About as many as the Chinese."

"Really? I don't believe it. Where?"

"Yesterday. In the paper. The *Los Angeles Times*." She studied him harshly. "Why do you keep shrugging?"

"I don't know." He forced himself not to do it again.

She shook her head. "Don't you care?"

After the War

1946

One afternoon, a year after their father died, the two Navarro boys marched into the village with their Tio Salvador. Emerging from the jungle, they helped carry a long bamboo pole horizontally between their shoulders from which a near naked Japanese man hung hog-tied from wrists and ankles: all he wore was soiled underwear covering his privates, which stuck to him like sodden banana leaves. Bits of tattered military uniform stuck to his skin, caked by mud, the angular bones of his emaciated body still visible beneath. He had been hiding in the jungle. Then hunted. His body was crisscrossed by bloody cuts, scrapes, bruises. His gaunt leg bone broken and crooked beneath his skinny flesh, as if it had been snapped and shifted, creating knobs and bumps. On closer look—a crowd was gathering and village boys ran up to poke at him—his knuckles appeared misshapen too. Yet his eyes opened, at the sound of the approaching Filipinos.

"Hoy! He's alive!"

Salvador wore a soiled khaki U.S.-issue uniform, but the brothers simply wore shorts and T-shirts dirtied by a month in the jungle, which stuck to their bodies like mud. The village boys looked at them with awe.

"Pepe and Betino captured a Japanese soldier in the jungle!" their cousins shouted.

Immediately the stories circulated: this Japanese had been left behind by his countrymen when his emperor surrendered. He had been forgotten, he didn't know the war was over, or he refused to surrender. The crowd grew angry at the man, angry at the particular slant in his eyes, at the stockiness of his torso and body, at the pleading in his pupils, and village boys began to prod at his eyes with sticks. Somebody brought out a curved bolo knife.

Then the boys pulled back from the naked man and stared at the brothers who had helped capture him. Betino had an angry glint in his eyes, but also a smirk; nobody was surprised by this, given all that the Japanese had done to his family. But his gentle older brother had his head bowed, looking at the ground not with the pride he seemed to deserve, but rather—and this was quite puzzling—a deep and painful blush.

Part Two

Mourning

Of all his siblings, Betino had the warmest feelings for Dina. She was like a daughter to him. After their father died, she took the loss especially hard and began sneaking into Betino's bed at night, afraid their father's soul would visit them; it was said that their mother had never wished to marry, dreamed of becoming a Carmelite, so Dina worried that his spirit lingered in this world, afraid that Camille would forget him and possibly even remarry. Betino reassured Dina that this was an impossible notion even for a soul to hold; everyone knew Camille would never do such an unfaithful thing as to marry again.

"But Papa might worry that Mommy will join a convent," Dina said.

"So?"

"If a widow joins a convent, then she marries Jesus. Then her soul can never rejoin with her dead husband in Heaven. Papa will come back to ask us to prevent Mommy from becoming a nun."

"That's ridiculous."

"No it's not, Kuya. I keep seeing a black dog outside our window. He looks at me and I can see in his eyes that it's Papa."

Betino told her it was just a dog but Dina would not listen, so he waited with her until it returned, the next evening, during a blood moon that hung like a reddened eye over the volcano across the coconut groves. The moon bathed the jungle foothills of Mt. Kawayan in pink light, which silhouetted the coconut trees' shaggy fronds, and the peasants believed its spring waters came from tears of the Virgin Mary and (if consumed with faith and love) had healing power.

The dog, which had been howling in a nearby alley, now looked at him intently, and indeed seemed to have a human presence.

"See!" Dina shouted to Betino, burying her head in his shoulder. She trembled against him.

"That's not Papa," he said, hiding his uncertainty.

He took this problem to a Jesuit at his school, because they frowned on superstition and scolded the Filipino students not to believe in ghosts, claiming this to be a pagan tradition left over from pre-Hispanic times and allowed to remain by corrupt Spanish clergy. The gentle Jesuit with his silver hair, Father Henderson from Illinois—who had been a schoolteacher before independence, then a missionary among Muslims in Mindanao and the Mountain People near Baguio—laughed and showed him a place in the New Testament where Jesus told the Pharisees that husbands and wives do not reunite in Heaven but are equally angels of God.

"Show this to your sister," he said. "Your deceased father has nothing to worry about."

"That proves nothing," Dina said to Betino after he had read to her the Biblical passage. "How would Papa know that?"

"Because he's dead."

"But he's not in Heaven yet."

"Dina, that dog is not Papa. This is not a Catholic idea."

She reluctantly promised to stop believing the dog was their father. The dog kept returning, however, and regarded them with pleading, lonely eyes. They seemed human, even to Betino. When they heard it howl at the moon the sound was mournful and human and sad, and Dina shivered beside him beneath the sheets.

Betino returned to the Jesuit father. "You should hear it howl, Father. It sounds human."

"Have you such little faith, child?" the Father snapped in frustration, stunning Betino who had never seen him angry before. "Didn't I show you what Jesus said in the Bible? Don't you people read or listen to anything we've been teaching you?"

Betino rebuked himself all day, could not concentrate during his classes, barely ate his mother's red paella at dinner whose spicy fragrance steamed his face. He called himself foolish, felt ashamed that he had had such a primitive and evil notion. Was even annoyed at Dina for having planted such a silly, native thought in his head. Yet that night the black dog returned, its ragged ribs showing in the porch light, looking at him like a lost soul, and something moved within him, and his hair lifted on the back of his neck.

He was disturbed at his lingering belief that this was, indeed his father. It was a temptation from Satan to his beliefs as a Catholic. He felt guilty at Communion, terrified as he took the host on his tongue. He forced his mother, who prayed to photographs of his father for the well-being of the family, to stop praying to dead relatives; he exaggerated and told her that the Jesuit father had said doing so was a mortal sin.

During the daytime he rid himself of his superstition, yet at night the black dog came to them, and Betino's certainty that its eyes were human returned. Dina cried and lay sleepless in his bed, listening to the melancholy howls in the darkness.

"Papa's lonely!" she cried.

All day his pretty sister looked tired and haggard, and her grades began to falter. He took pity on her and wished to help. He had to put a stop to this.

This is a test from God, he decided. A test of my faith.

He knew what he had to do, to protect his sister and prove his faith, like Peter before the second crowing cock.

That evening the melancholy howls bathed the coconut valley like the mournful voices of Duarte Lobo's Requiem for Six Voices, a choral piece which always stunned Betino with its sad beauty as sung within St. Sebastian's Moorish arches, and he removed Dina's clutching hands from his arms and stood. He headed for the door.

She sat up. "Where are you going?" she said.

"Outside."

"Are you crazy?"

"If you are so certain this is Papa, why should I be afraid of my own father?"

"But he's a spirit."

"Nonsense," he said. "This must stop."

His sister's frightened face haunted his mind as he stepped into the alleyway behind the house. He crouched behind a trash can and waited: moonlight bathed the south-facing houses and cast shadows over the road. One shadow began moving, and he squinted and saw that it was the black dog. He expected it to go to the window, as was its routine, but it came directly to him, as if it knew him, and looked at him with its human eyes.

"Papa?" he said.

The dog did not answer, but nor did it beg from him like most dogs. Even in the dim light he could see the shadows along its bony ribs. As it regarded him, the emaciated legs trembled unsteadily, its knobby elbows almost threadbare.

He opened his coat and pulled out his father's weapon, a Colt .45 the man had purchased from an American soldier who claimed to have used it against Muslims in Mindanao, and Betino pointed it at the dog. Its tail wagged as it looked at him trustfully, and Betino set his finger against the cold trigger and then he pulled it and watched the dog collapse. It lay there whining. It looked surprised. It looked up at Betino in confusion. Betino bent over and lay a hand on its mangy stomach, felt its ribs through the starved skin, and the warm liquid running on his hand. He comforted the dog who, strangely, did not try to snap at him. Betino did not have the heart to finish it off and he waited there for a very long time.

When he returned to his bedroom, Dina looked up at him with panic. She held silver rosary beads in her hands.

"Bino, what did you do?" she cried.

He looked down at his red hands. They were streaked also by wet soil.

"Bino? What did you do?"

He moved to the window and listened to the wild dogs howling at the base of Mt. Kawayan, where flowed the healing waters.

"I have saved us from ourselves," he said.

Anesthesia

I

When Dina's family called from the Philippines–to suggest that her brother join Dina and her husband in Los Angeles–she hesitated.

"Our apartment is small," she said and glanced from the kitchenette counter to the sunny living room windows, which glistened with steam from cooking rice. "Where would he stay?"

"He can sleep on your mother's bedroom floor," Tita Candida said.

"On her floor."

"He can help take care of her."

"But Mommy's not all that frail."

"Come on, Dina! Pepe doesn't like living in your older brother's house. You know how humiliated he feels, surrounded by Betino's family and without a purpose or job."

Dina tensed; she tapped her husband's reading glasses against her delaminating countertop, clicking its fading orange surface, not knowing how to explain her worry: that her American husband might feel taken advantage of. Only three years ago her mother had moved into this crowded two-bedroom apartment with their noisy kids, and her sister had spent six months on the couch. Even now, her children's thumping and shouting came muted through the bedroom door.

"Betino has a much larger house than our apartment," Dina said. "Remember, people here don't live crowded together the way they do in Manila."

"*Dina*," her *tita* said and made a brisk clicking noise with her tongue. "Don't you love your brother?"

He arrived at LAX two months later, along with several enormous *balikbayan* boxes. Dina's children got excited and believed her brother owned many belongings, but when they opened the boxes everything inside was gifts for family. Filipino candies. Chocolates. Saint dolls and a carved Infant of Prague from the Visayas wrapped in damp newspaper shavings that filled the room with strange scents and musk. Pepe had brought almost nothing of his own.

He slept on Mommy's floor that night. The next morning he walked her down the steep front stairs to church, for her daily Mass, then cooked her Filipino foods for lunch.

"I'll walk your children home from school," he said. He was pulling groceries from crinkling plastic bags.

"You don't have to do that, Pepe."

"Yes, yes. I want to."

"Are you sure?"

He nodded with his gentle smile.

"*O siya.* Thank you, Pepe. It'll actually save us money. I won't have to take the time off work to get them."

He took a special liking to her boy, Ben ("Twig"), who had muscle hypotonia and still could not walk even at five. Pepe would walk him down the steep outdoor stairway that descended to the common courtyard. There he sat the child on the grass beside a utility blanket, placed tools on it, and worked at restoring Seth's old Indian motorcycle that had gathered rust in the backyard over a decade of exposure to salty Santa Monica Bay fog and Pacific Ocean rains. He named for the boy the tools and parts and tried to teach him how the engine should work.

～✦～

Two weeks passed. Her husband watched through the blinds slats as Pepe led Mommy down the dewy outdoor stairs, gripping her elbow.

"Is your brother planning to walk your mother to church every single morning?" Seth said.

"The front steps are steep," she said.

"Well sure, but your mother isn't all that old," he said. "We can put down traction. She's only a year older than my mother, and you know how Mom lives in that old house all alone in Illinois, and won't even let me clean out her gutters. She claims that being self-reliant is what keeps her from getting old too fast."

"Well, my mother likes having him take care of her," Dina said tightly, pinching her jacket cuff, sharpening the crease.

"It just seems that he doesn't have much time for himself," he said.

"He feels obliged to help her," she said.

Their smallest boy was on the floor nearby, playing with a plastic castle set, and glanced up. "Mom, when is Tito Pepe going to find his own apartment?" he asked.

"I told you honey, he's staying with us."

"You mean, like, for forever?"

Dina shifted on her feet.

Her husband let down the window blinds that clattered and he mussed Ben's hair. "He's going to stay with us as long as he wants to, Twig buddy, to help out with your grandmother."

Ben looked at them with puzzled eyes, but shrugged and turned back to his toy set.

One evening at bath time, as Dina tried to keep shampoo out of Ben's eyes while rinsing his hair, her son said, "Is Tito Pepe going to live with us because he's missing those fingers on his left hand?"

Dina regarded him. (What strange thoughts children had!) "Of course not, Twig," she said, using the affectionate nickname for him that was only used within the family. "He's staying with us to help out with your Lola Camille. He's staying with us because he's family."

Ben nodded and looked down. He watched water run over his thin waist, which was about two-thirds as large as those of most children his age. Sometimes she looked at the narrowness of his body, the jutted hip and tapered legs, and felt a creeping surge of panic, a sort of realization that she was in willful denial, though it usually passed with a smile from the boy, or a laugh. He looked up at her again. "Why does Tito Pepe only have three fingers on that hand?"

"That happened during the war."

"You mean when the Japanese were there?"

"Yes."

"How'd it happen?"

"I don't know."

"How can you not know? He's your brother."

"He's a very private person," she said. "But it happened when he was a guerrilla soldier."

"Pepe was a soldier?" Ben said. "Why didn't you tell me?"

"I have. You kids weren't interested."

"He doesn't seem like one. He seems so quiet."

"Quiet people can be soldiers too," she said; her voice sounded sharper than intended, and her son's shoulders tensed beneath her soaping hands; he was a quiet boy and she worried over him and even hoped her stoic brother could become a role model. Sometimes she worried that his developmental "delay" was really more like developmental "disorder." She worried that if he didn't catch up fast enough with the other kids he'd need to be taken care of by her forever. Sometimes she secretly didn't mind the thought. But she knew such thinking was selfish, and found that she could squeeze it out of her mind by brooding over what would happen to him when she and Seth died.

She said, "Just because someone is self-deprecatory and doesn't brag, doesn't mean they aren't capable of being respected in life, Twig."

Her son stared at the soapy water pooling about the drain: she'd been a bit too obvious.

Dina wanted her children to respect the quietness of her brother so much that it gnawed at her insides like a worm. She prodded Pepe to apply for clerical office jobs—after all, he held a college degree from the Ateneo—but he'd instead found part-time night work as a custodian, paid under the table without benefits, which she knew he only took due to shyness and modesty. She tried to set him up on a couple of dates, but that predictably didn't work: he refused, obviously mortified by the very idea.

After finishing the bath, she called her older son Matt to come in and help carry his brother out of the tub. Matt gripped Ben from behind the shoulders, while Dina held Ben's damp ankles and walked backward into her room, worrying that a boy Ben's age should not have to be seen naked by his brother. They set him on her bedspread, and Matt returned to his homework in the kitchenette. Dina tugged Ben's pajamas on.

She showed Ben and Becca several photographs she kept in a box beneath her bed, including an old black-and-white of her brother as a young teenager in ragged khaki military garb. Pepe stood beside several older soldiers, Filipinos and Americans both, before some thatched huts and banana trees. She hadn't seen this picture in ages. The soldiers all had dirty faces, gaunt and skeletal, and ripped-up clothes that bunched over their shoulders. Their arms and necks emaciated with raised veins. It was taken after a period of intense fighting and slaughter. The men all looked at the camera—at you—with weak and celebratory and haunted eyes.

"He looks so young, Mom," Becca said. The girl slid the photographs around on the quilted bedspread like a rare hand of cards.

"Yes, he was still a child," Dina said.

"Why are the Filipinos and the American soldiers wearing the same uniforms?" said Ben, who studied the photograph intently.

Dina looked away and said, "It had made sense then."

She did not tell them about the time Japanese soldiers had come through the village near Kawayan, and taken a pregnant girl and slit open her belly and tossed the unborn child up and then raised a bayonet to catch it coming down. She did not tell them about the neighboring hacienda mansion that had been so opulent and how the family were allowed to live in one wing there, while the officers used the others, rumored to be used for interrogations (the servants were said to have heard screaming; and when the Japanese fled and the townsfolk went inside, they found torture equipment and dried blood splattered on the walls). She did not tell them about how truly angry everyone was after the war, how even two years later some fishermen from the hacienda spotted a Japanese fishing boat and her uncles went out and burned it. In the evening, from the beach, you could see it out on the black ocean, like a bonfire aglow in the distant dark. They came back through the local village carrying Japanese who could be fishermen tied like pigs from bamboo sticks, charred, even their eyelids seared off, their clothes blackened and soggy . . . and how the next day, the sand was speckled by tiny pieces of charred driftwood, little black puddles, thin layers of drifted ash.

Later, wading at the beach, Becca asked, "But if your brother was such a guerrilla soldier, how come he's afraid of grown-up people in Los Angeles?"

"He's not afraid of people," Dina said curtly, though she turned aside. They stood on the wet sand of Leo Cabrillo, as frigid water lapped at their ankles, leaving fizzling foam behind. Becca wore huge sunglasses with pink plastic rims that were popular with her bratty middle school classmates at the time.

"You could have fooled me," Becca said.

"I don't know what you're talking about."

"Soldiers meet other grown-up people's eyes. And he disappears from the apartment whenever we have guests, or hides in his room."

"Don't be ridiculous," Dina said.

"How am I being ridiculous?"

"Not everyone loves parties, young lady. You should not be surprised when you find, later in life, that not everyone in this world loves silly gossips and endless talk."

"Oh please."

II

Last year her son's pediatric neurologist suggested that Ben might have a metabolic disorder. That if this was true it would explain his limp muscles, small stature, and hypersensitive responses to auditory stimulation. But the tests available to them had come out inconclusive. They couldn't know for sure.

"What is this, I have never heard of it?" she asked.

"It's rare," the doctor replied vaguely.

She looked it up in the university library. She read words like *progressive* and *incurable*. She read words like *cardiomyopathy* and *spastic paracesis*. She read words like *sensory input hypersensitivity* and *neural dysfunction*. She read words like *developmental delay, mitochondrial cytopathy*, and *mental retardation*.

"One doctor said they all have mental retardation," she told the neurologist.

"What doctor?"

"Someone writing in a parent support group newsletter."

"You shouldn't read informal newsletters, unless you can take it with a grain of salt." He shook his head. He wore a yellow smiley face button pinned to his white lapel, and it sagged forward as if making a bow. "You get all sorts of hysterical parents and people writing in with the worse cases," he added.

"So some people don't have it so badly?"

"Probably. Think about it. If someone has it only mildly, they are going to be undiagnosed," he said. "We don't know about them. They aren't going to make it into the literature."

She went home. She tried not to look at her stack of xeroxes and checked-out books and medical magazines. She paced, sat at the table, stood, and paced again. Don't think about it. Don't go there. Don't read it. Your boy might, apparently, be one of the lucky ones who didn't make it into the literature. So why read the literature? She went to her desk. Flipped open the literature. One parent recommended looking into your family for signs of mild symptoms of the disorder—undiagnosed cases—aunts with bad hips, grandmothers with heat intolerance, cousins clumsy at sports.

She slammed the book shut. On the desk was a black-and-white family photograph, from the Philippines, with Pepe standing humbly to the side, his face saggy, his eyes anxious even at about age eight. She lay it facedown.

"Perhaps I have it," she told the neurologist. "I've never been good at sports."

"You don't have it," he said. "Look at you. You can stand, you can walk."

"Perhaps I have heat intolerance."

"You're from the Philippines. That's a tropical country."

"Yes, and I always feel tired there."

"I come from Georgia. Take my word, everyone does in humid air."

"Perhaps it runs in my family. Perhaps it's my fault. I read one parent who said her doctor said her grandmother and aunts must have had it and nobody realized. All because they can't stay under the sun or exercise. They get hot, grow limp, sweat."

"I told you not to look at those newsletters."

"I'm sorry, Doctor." She glanced at her lap, then said, "But if I have it and nobody notices, then maybe nobody will notice Ben has it later in life. He could have it only a little and then it will get better."

He pinched his black gabardines at the crease over his knee, then brushed at it as if he'd seen a fly.

She said, "So it's possible Ben has it only a little and will get better?"

He paused. "It's progressive."

"What does that mean? Progressive. It sounds like a good thing. That it gets better."

"Theoretically it means it only gets worse. But sometimes it just sort of plateaus for a long time. And we do have treatments. We can treat symptoms with the same therapies used for multiple sclerosis, muscular dystrophy, cerebral palsy; you know, things like antiseizure drugs, drugs for cardiac myopathy."

Dina had gripped her chair arms very tightly. She realized a fingernail had cracked.

"Maybe he's just shy," she said.

"Could be." He averted his eyes.

"And it's possible even if he has it he'll just be sensitive, right?"

"Well—and perhaps a bit clumsy."

She shook her head. She rubbed her face against her sleeve. "I don't care about clumsy," she said. "I can love clumsy. I don't want people to pick on him. That would be painful. People—they can be so cruel."

"Look, Dina—either way, the main thing is for him to have confidence. Be a good example. Surround him with confident role models." The doctor self-consciously straightened in his seat. "I think you'll find that, as with anybody, people respond to you the way you think about yourself."

She noticed things about Pepe. How he left Seth's motorcycle parts all over the carport floor, an eyesore for the neighbors, as if they still lived in Manila. How he picked up her kids in those greasy old linen pants with the frayed cuffs—their teacher even called her one afternoon to make sure that the man waiting outside for them was really her brother. *He says he's their uncle, but he looks a bit like a homeless person, Miss Katie said. Maybe it would be best if you spoke on the phone with this man just to make sure it's him.*

She found her brother in the alleyway, kneeling on the asphalt, working on her husband's motorcycle.

"Pepe."

He looked up and gave his gentle smile. "Yes?"

"Seth's brother and his wife are coming next week."

He stood, rubbed his greasy hands on his pants. "When are they arriving? I will pick them up at the airport."

"*Salamat*, Pepe, but you don't need to do that."

"I want to."

"Seth is going to pick them up."

"He wants to?"

"Yes."

He nodded. They went through this conversation each time one of Seth's relatives came to town. "Let them sleep in my bed. I'll sleep on the floor."

71

"That's okay, they're going to stay in a hotel."

"I insist."

"They want to," she lied. In truth, Seth always asked his relatives to stay in motels because the apartment was so crowded with her relatives. Sometimes her mother invited siblings, uncles, aunts, cousins to visit from the Philippines and stay in her room for weeks at a time.

"Okay," Pepe finally relented.

She asked him if he could clear up the carport before they arrived. He blushed as he nodded. An awkward moment passed. She took a breath and said, "And perhaps we can go shopping at JCPenney tomorrow."

"Why?"

"To buy you some new clothes."

He shook his head. "I don't need them," he said, apparently not wanting to spend the money.

"It's okay, I'll buy them."

"No, no."

She looked over his greasy gray pants, with the frayed belt loops and cuffs, the oil-stained shirt, and felt sudden irritation. "Pepe," she said, "the children's new schoolteacher called me the other day. She didn't think you were my brother and didn't want to let the children go home with you."

Her brother's face changed. His laugh lines crinkled, squeezed as he looked at her.

"Pepe, I think it's the motorcycle grease on your pants, is all," she added awkwardly, her face growing hot. "He shoved his hands into his pockets. "Okay, I will buy some pants."

"I'll take you now."

"No, I can go alone."

"You need a woman to help you choose, Pepe. I'm coming with you."

Her brother flinched—as if she'd implied that he should have a wife—and she wondered about what a terrible sister she was being, if she'd become one of those impatient insensitive people she had always avoided, and never wanted to become.

She led him through the makeup counters to the men's section, his hands boyishly in his pockets, nervously looking around. He nearly tripped when his shoulder caught a clothes rack. A browsing couple noticed and Dina flushed. She gathered some chinos and short-sleeved button-down shirts and made him try them on. He didn't want to come out of the dressing room, but she insisted he let her see. She reached into the curtain and grabbed his hand. He emerged, avoiding her eyes and the mirror that held his reflection. She said, "Step into the light, Pepe. That's better. Turn around so I can see how it fits."

He hesitated, but did so.

His creases were as sharp as the folds of a boy's paper airplane, at the pleats, the cuffs, down from the knees.

"*Guapo*," she said.

He smiled gently, trustfully, which made her cringe and blush: she did not tell him the real reason she wanted to buy him new clothes, that she wanted her husband's relatives to give him the respect he deserved.

Seth's brother and sister-in-law visited from Ohio and stayed at a motel because the apartment was so crowded with Dina's relatives. The couple chose a place four blocks away so they could walk over for meals.

They ate at the kitchenette table with the kids and Dina's mother. Pepe ate his food alone in his bedroom, and never met their eyes when he emerged to use the bathroom. The gossipy wife, Judith, traded curious glances with her husband. Dina fiddled with the table flowers as if they needed rearranging.

The next day at the Universal Studios Tour, as they rode in a bumpy open-air tram, Judith asked Seth what Pepe did for a living. Seth said he took care of his mother.

Judith raised her brows. "Really?" she said. She held her yellow floppy hat in place as their tram bounced downhill.

"He likes to care for her," Seth said. "It's sort of a, well, Filipino cultural thing. They often assign one of the grown children to take care of the elderly parents."

"So he doesn't work?"

"He has a part-time job."

"But what does he do for medical insurance?"

"Come on, honey," Seth's brother said with an embarrassed chuckle, elbowing his wife gently and nodding toward Dina.

The sun beat on Dina's face. The tram rattled over a speed bump and she steadied herself by shifting on her warm fiberglass seat.

"He says he doesn't need it," she said. "After all, most people don't have such luxuries in the Philippines."

"Oh, well, that's very nice of him," Judith said and smiled at her brightly. "To take care of your mother."

Dina held her sweaty metal handle for balance. "Yes it is," she said.

The woman smiled back, but Dina could read in her eyes what she was thinking, *Your relatives are leeching off you and your husband. This is America, not the Philippines. But I guess it's none of my business if Seth doesn't feel like he's being taken advantage of by a brother-in-law who could be out there in the world, trying to find decent work, and a mother-in-law who has never worked a day in her life and sits praying with her rosaries and idols for hours every day.*

Doubtless, she would bring tales back to Ohio to tell the extended family as dinner gossip.

That evening she and her husband lay reading in bed. It creaked as Seth turned to her. "Did your brother really say that he didn't want medical insurance?"

"No."

"Maybe we should get some for him."

"We can't afford it," she said. "Look, it's sweet of you to care. I know you feel guilty—because you want to be a good person. But really, none of my relatives back in Manila have such things. You're being generous just to house him."

"I just feel responsible."

"By that logic we should send all our spare money back to the Philippines," she said. "Look, he doesn't expect it. You're a schoolteacher. We have young children."

He smoothed the bedspread where it lumped over his knees. "Yeah, I guess I see your point," he said.

He smoothed the bedspread where it lumped over his knees. "Yeah, I guess I see your point," he said.

At the Third Street Promenade, walking through the crowd along the shops, she noticed Ben slouching in his stroller in what seemed like an exaggerated imitation of a monk.

"Why are you sitting like that, Twig?" she said.

"Like what?"

"Slouched."

He seemed unconcerned. "I'm being humble. Like a saint."

"Well, sit up straight. People are staring."

He shook his head. "I'm sitting like Tito Pepe," he said and faced forward as she turned them into a bookstore. A woman behind the register smiled down at him, but Dina noticed that Ben had bowed his head and lifted his hand to shield his eyes.

III

She noticed bloodstains on one of her brother's white undershirts as she collected clothes from the hampers to do laundry, peeling them apart to toss into separate piles. She waited for her brother on the landing, sitting on the old wicker gliding chair she'd bought while she was nursing Becca, and confronted him when he returned from walking her kids to school.

"What's this?" she said holding out the shirt.

"Sorry," Pepe said. "Is it too dirty to clean?"

"Is this blood?"

"Yes."

"Are you hurt?"

"No," he said. "It's just an old injury."

"Show me."

"It's only a little blood."

"Pepe."

He sighed and unbuttoned his outer shirt and then tugged his under-shirt out of his pants and lifted the bottom. There was an old wide scar on his abdomen—Dina remembered it now, from the war—that looked like the cut of a woman's C-section, and he had bandages over the middle part of it soaked in blood.

"Pepe, what's that?"

"It came open."

"And you just stuck a bandage on it?"

"I sewed it up."

"We need to get you to a doctor."

"I don't need one."

"Yes you do."

"Will it be expensive?"

"We'll get you medical coverage. I should've gotten you some be-fore."

"How much will it cost?"

"You're a vet. We'll get it from the VA office."

"No."

"What do you mean, no?"

"I wasn't a U.S. soldier."

"Don't talk crap. Of course you were. We'll explain it to them."

Her brother looked nervous. He shook his head: "I don't think so."

"Ben's Ninong Maning was a guerrilla soldier and he gets benefits," she said.

"He was a Philippine Scout. I was just a boy."

"I insist, Pepe. I'll do the talking."

They went to the Veteran's Administration campus Maning told her about, rather than the closest one, and drove around until they discov-ered the building, and they parked far away and walked there and wan-dered the huge building looking for the room with the right number. The numbers seemed to be all out of order here, and the floors divided strangely into different wings, and they spent fifteen minutes wandering the corridors before they found the room.

There were various desks and windows with employees looking bored behind them, and long lines before each one that crowded the enormous room.

"This is it," Dina said.

"Who do we talk to?"

"I don't know."

"There are so many lines."

"Let's ask someone," Dina said.

"Let's just go."

"Don't be silly." She went up to one counter and several people in line glanced at her with irritation. The clerk told her she had to wait in line.

"But I don't know which line to wait in," she explained. "That's what I want to ask."

"You need to wait in that line over there to ask," the woman said pointing.

"But it's so long."

"You gotta take your turn."

Dina backed up and returned to Pepe. "We have to wait in that line over there."

"They will give us the form?"

"No, they'll tell us how to get it."

They walked out of the room into the hallway to find the end of the line and they found it and stood beneath a broken flickering fluorescent light, behind a man with no arm. It moved very slowly. The corridor smelled of human sweat. They waited an hour and a half and got to the black woman who worked the window.

"Excuse me, Ma'am. We need to find the form for my brother to fill out to get his medical benefits."

She looked at Pepe.

"He's a veteran," Dina explained.

"Where'd you fight?"

"In the Philippines," he said.

"You don't sound American."

"I'm a legal resident."

"Listen, just 'cause you're a veteran of another country don't mean you get to get medical benefits here."

Pepe looked at Dina as if to say *let's please just leave*, but she gave him a nudge.

"We were a U.S. territory," he said. "I was a part of the U.S. Army."

The woman looked at him as if he were crazy. "You got papers to show this?"

"I have an affidavit."

"An affidavit? From who?"

Pepe blushed. He opened his manila envelope and pulled out several yellowed pieces of paper. She frowned but took them from him.

She spread the pages out on her desk and shook her head and she chuckled and looked up again. "This is from a priest."

"He was my teacher at college."

"All it says is that you were a guerrilla soldier and allied with Americans against the Japanese."

Pepe said nothing.

Dina stepped forward. "Guerrilla soldiers were inducted into the U.S. Army by President Roosevelt," she said. "He said we should be proud of them."

The woman turned to the man at the next desk and tapped his shoulder. "Listen here. Look at this. It's an affidavit from a priest."

They began laughing.

"Excuse me," Dina said.

They continued to laugh.

Pepe said, "Let's just go."

"Excuse me, but you're being rude," she said to the clerks.

A man behind them in line had been impatiently staring at them and shaking his head. He said, "Look lady, you're holding the line up. They're not going to give your brother anything because he wasn't an American soldier. It's hot in here. You're wasting my time, and the time of the people behind me."

"This is none of your business," she said to the man.

"Oh yes it is. I've been waiting in this line for two goddamn motherfucking hours and have to pick up my kids from school. So don't tell me this isn't my business, you fucking bargirl cunt."

Pepe, who had taken her arm and been trying to pull her toward the door, suddenly let go of her elbow and threw a punch at the man's face. It deflected off his fleshy chin and sounded like a slap. He punched back and Dina yelled and a security guard and two other men jumped in and pulled them apart. She noticed blood on the other man's neck and face, and that it came from his mangled ear. She followed them as they dragged her brother outside and shoved him onto the front concrete steps. He stumbled forward but did not fall.

"Oh Pepe, are you hurt?" She went up and touched his face.

"No."

"But they hit you in the face."

"It wasn't hard."

She could see that his face looked all right, just a small cut on his lip with a little blood. It was shiny in the sunlight; his teeth tinted a light pink, gathered at the gums as if he'd flossed overvigorously after long neglect. But as they walked to the car and he leaned on her she felt his shirt and it was damp at his stomach, warm.

"I'm sorry," she cried. "You're bleeding."

"It doesn't hurt."

"Let's go to my husband's doctor. Seth'll pay."

"No, no," he refused.

"But you're my brother," she said. "And you're hurt."

He tried to tell her more things as he began to shake his head. She turned away, pressed her hands against her ears and refused to listen.

The doctor told Dina, as she was paying the bill, that her brother had done a remarkable job of stitching his own wound. "Only next time make sure he comes in here," he said, and glanced at Pepe with a chuckle and unrequited wink. "I can't guarantee I'll do a better job of it, but I promise you I'll use something to ease the pain."

Unacknowledged

I

During the year I entered junior high, my mother convinced my father to import a maid from the Philippines. She arranged for her brother, Betino, who still lived in Manila, to send one over to us; Father mailed him a check to bribe the customs officials on the Asian side and to purchase a fake visa for the agents here in Los Angeles. To get ready for the maid, we cleared out our musty garage, with its odor of stale dust and ancient grease. Father and my older brother, Matt, and I put up drywall and laid in plywood floors and carpeting, and we bought a futon for the maid to sleep on. Father parked the cars on the streets. We painted the walls a cream color, which Father thought would be more cheerful than stark white, but he stared at the bare walls, the garage door opened to air out the smell of paint, and frowned. "It's not good enough," he said, and shook his head. Then he asked Inay to help him decorate the room. "It's too depressing to live in."

She laughed and told him the room was fine, that it was far nicer than the shanties most urban Filipinos lived in, or the nipa huts you found out in the countryside. Father was from the Midwest and had only lived in nice areas of Palawan, a beachy outpost popular with European scuba divers and tourists, where he worked as a teacher, had met our mother, and where Matt and Becca and I were born.

Becca and I cleared out the car trunks to make room for the maid's luggage, and we drove to the airport in a caravan of two cars–Father and Matt behind the steering wheels. We'd never had a live-in maid before, at least not since we left the Philippines when I was three. Here in California, my parents had not been able to afford one, not on my father's schoolteacher salary. Their income then was strained by unusual costs. Inay's brother and mother lived with us in a cramped apartment at the time. A parade of visiting relatives would arrive from the Philippines, staying with us for weeks, eating our food, using up gas on trips to Disneyland and other tourist spots across the state. And my parents spent a great deal of money on my medical care, my copays and wheelchairs and braces and ramps, something I overheard them whispering about through a closed door. Recently, however, to their relief, Father finally got promoted to assistant principal, and we moved into a house.

"What's this maid like?" Becca asked her.

Startled out of her thoughts, Inay turned to my sister: "Your Tito Betino says she's very hardworking and responsible. A good person."

"Is she one of his maids?"

"No." Inay frowned. She wanted one of her brother's own maids—strictly trained by his wife Millie—but Tito Betino insisted none were available. "He says this one is very professional."

Father was quiet this whole time. He didn't believe people needed maids (he came from a Midwestern family of factory workers and farmers), and always frowned at her use of that word (preferring *housekeeper*), but Inay would make fun of him and tell him to make his own burgers at McDonald's and to bus his own tables at restaurants if he did not like division of labor. And anyway, he was not the one who did most of the housework.

~~~

According to Inay, even lower-middle-class people had maids in the Philippines. Each time we went to visit Tito Betino, we stayed at his house and were looked after by four maids, a houseboy, and three chauffeurs, who drove our uncle, aunt, and cousins—Malaya and Juliet—around. The drivers took us to the shopping centers, where they dropped us off at the entrance; then they would wait at a curb nearby, parked illegally in a car that baked in the wrenchingly hot sun, keeping an eye on the mall entrance so that as soon as we stepped outside they could hurry over and pick us up. One time our aunt came, too. The driver didn't immediately see us emerge, causing Tita Millie to frown. She gave the man a huge scolding in front of us kids.

At family meals the maids would hover behind us, filling our glasses, serving us from dishes we could easily have reached ourselves, fanning flies away with huge banana fronds as if we were Egyptian royalty in the old MGM movies our Midwestern father liked to watch.

Inay was much more circumspect about the whole situation. Occasionally her sister-in-law would scold a maid in front of us, driving the poor girl to look at the ground as Millie told her how incompetent she was, stupid and inconsiderate, and later, privately, Inay would criticize that behavior. "There's no excuse for Millie to be scolding her maids so harshly," she said. "That kind of humiliation is hardly Catholic. Not all rich Filipinos treat their employees that way just because they're poor and can't afford to quit. I hope you kids don't learn bad habits from seeing her do this."

"Of course we wouldn't, Mom," Becca said, frowning, offended.

Inay ignored her and continued, "Rich people here walk all over their help, because the poor people are so desperate for work. If we treat them even twice as nice as Millie does, they'll be supergrateful, not like the spoiled housekeepers you find in America. No matter how much you pay them, they feel they deserve more." She shook her head. "Americans are so spoiled," she added and glanced pointedly at Becca, who frowned and pushed her bangs off her eyes, her metal wrist bangles jangling down her skinny arm almost to her elbow crook.

After we returned to Los Angeles, our mother began her campaign to convince her brother to send over one of his well-trained maids—a girl so yelled-at and overworked she'd be thankful to be in our home. As the woman's arrival date neared, our house grew thick with excitement. My sister told her friends at school we'd be getting one of our rich Filipino uncle's maids. For her, this was an opportunity to distinguish us from the masses of poor Filipinos you saw in California, if you noticed

Filipinos at all. Becca was sensitive to what most people thought of Filipinos, and hated being lumped together with mail-order brides and prostitutes and farm laborers and domestic help, who were thought of as so lowly that they were routinely beaten by their Saudi Arabian and Singaporean masters, or so we heard on television. Her friends related the condescending sneer a new Hong Kong girl made at school when she found out Becca was a Filipina ("Oh, yes, we get a lot of cheap Filipino laborers in Hong Kong, because local workers are so expensive," she scoffed), and Becca always avoided the half-Filipino girl whose father had been a soldier based in Subic Bay and reputedly married her bar-girl mother. One former friend from the tennis team, after falling out with Becca, called her a "Filipina barwhorelovechildmonkey" in front of teammates, causing Becca to leave the court in tears. Becca told our classmates that it was *wrong* for anyone to lump all Filipinos together. She always pointed to the fact that our great-great-granduncle was a famous poet and martyr, who had also been a surgeon in Europe, and that her round eyes came from Spanish blood. At other times she lied and told people we were actually of Chinese ancestry, descended from Sino traders of high intelligence and an ancient written culture who settled in the Visayan Islands south of Luzon.

<hr/>

We drove to the airport together, and stood behind the rope watching the passengers swarm out of customs, as Matt held up a cardboard sign with Inay's maiden name written in red felt-tip letters. We scoured all the women's faces, to see if they were looking for us, for any eyes that found our sign and showed recognition. Time and again people looked it over, but kept going. Finally, a fat, pleasant-faced woman saw the sign and her eyes brightened, still a bit apprehensive, but she smiled as she waddled over toward us.

"That must be her," Matt said.

Inay eagerly looked for her. Suddenly Inay's expression changed; she squeezed my wrist, her fingernails biting deep. "Oh, I can't believe it."

"*What?*" Becca said.

Inay bit her lip, shaking her head, looking aside. "I can't believe my brother did this to us."

"What, Mom—would you *please* tell us what you're talking about?"

And then we noticed the teenage girl behind the maid, shyly following her mother with her eyes focused on the floor. She was maybe fourteen, fifteen—in a knee-length dress that hugged her slender figure, showing an outline of her hipbones, and wore cranberry lipstick.

Becca tensed and turned to our mother: "Who's *that*?"

Inay did not answer her, but simply shook her head.

What she wouldn't tell us, but which we discovered later—through the gossip network of cousins—was that this woman had been the mistress of Inay's deceased uncle—Lolo Bentong—and that the girl was their fifteen-year-old illegitimate daughter. On the drive home, our parents were grim and silent. Our father must have felt betrayed and taken advantage of. Inay sensed this; she was also seething at her brother.

Apparently my uncle had decided on his own that we would take care of this mistress and her illegitimate daughter, because of irresponsible Lolo Bentong's sins. But Father was an American, already providing for my widowed maternal grandmother who, at times, lived in our home. This "mistress" was actually something of a third wife, but she'd inherited nothing because Bentong's first wife (though long separated) was the only one recognized by the Catholic Church there because divorce was illegal.

Risa kept smiling at us, nervously, glancing at our parents in the front seats. The daughter, Teresa, was frail and pretty and sat squashed against the door, her thin shoulders hunched together, her cheap handbag hugged protectively on her lap. She stared out the window. As much as I was drawn to her enormous black eyes, I could barely look at her—I was so afraid—but my brother couldn't help regarding her. I'd seen that look on Matt before—whenever he saw something he wanted to protect: a wounded animal, a new scrawny kid at school, me. Even now that I no longer routinely needed a wheelchair or walker, and only sometimes used canes, he often walked beside me in public, furtively looking around for signs of staring or mocking eyes, especially when other kids were around.

That night our new maid slept on the garage bed, the daughter on the floor, their twine-wrapped *balikbayan* boxes pushed against the wall. I went to the kitchen, pretending to get milk, and listened to their muffled Tagalog whispers through the door. I could no longer understand the language, at least when spoken with their heavy ("deep") rural accents, but their tones were hushed and anxious. I took it the daughter was unhappy, and the mother only wanted her to quiet down.

II

At breakfast, as the mother served us eggs, we sat restlessly and quietly—unaccustomed to all this sitting.

The daughter was sitting outside, grim as she poked at her own sorry breakfast of leftover, coagulated eggs; her mother had given her the ones with broken yokes and saved the whole ones for us.

Matt kept going up to the window. He would watch her, shake his head, and return to our table. He wouldn't answer when Inay or Father tried to engage him in conversation. Each time he went to the window, it made all of us nervous, and even the girl's mother paced anxiously about the room whenever he showed concern.

Though he was already nearsighted from reading too much and looked bookish in his wire-rimmed glasses, my brother was also large, a hapkido black belt and member of the varsity soccer team. When I first entered Westwind School, a new boy in my class taunted me about my purple "girly" backpack (Inay had bought it for me on clearance, and refused to spend the money on a new one in a different color) and took my lunch money. The next day, I used a wheelchair, as I did on heat-wave days because extreme temperatures sapped my energy and I was weakened without lunch. Matt heard about this; enraged, he sought the bully out and came upon him in a nearby alleyway after school, with a couple of friends from the soccer team. They beat the boy to the asphalt, kicked his ribs in, and dislocated the boy's shoulder, and then retrieved my lunch money from the kid's pocket.

When Matt came home with a bruised face, suspended from class, Inay was angry with him. He'd gotten into a number of fights in elementary school, and developed problems with his grades; he seemed to be moving in a bad direction then, but she was strict, lecturing him and setting up rules and chores and bringing him to a streetwise Paulist priest who tutored him in moral philosophy and made him read the biographies of kindhearted men. She'd hired tutors and got him to calm down and even gain entrance into a private school fashionable with the children of movie industry people, Westwind for the Arts and Sciences. So she was disappointed, worried he would turn bad again, though when I told her why Matt had beaten up that boy she looked conflicted and even, if reluctantly, proud. It was easy for her to be proud of my brother, and I knew he was her favorite.

While Inay showed our new maid her duties around the house, the daughter remained outside, reading a book in English; Teresa seemed to be more educated than her mother, who only spoke deep Tagalog. The girl sat there all afternoon. Becca and I would go outside and sit on chairs across the lawn, reading our own books, but only Matt went up to her. He offered her iced tea and cookies, and though she at first declined, on his third try she accepted one cookie—embarrassed—then bowed her head and took a bite.

He returned to us.

"Why's she just sitting around out there?" Becca said, looking bothered.

"I think she doesn't know what else to do."

"She could help her mother."

"I don't think so."

"Why not?"

"That's not her job," he said, and his eyes steadied on our sister. "We're not paying them two salaries, Becca."

She blushed and glanced down, then looked up at him again. "So am I supposed to entertain her, or what?"

"That would be up to you."

My sister peered sheepishly over at the girl. Teresa was probably older than Becca by a year, but seemed both shyer and yet mysteriously far older. She wore a thin dress that accentuated her figure and pantyhose that only came up to her calves, like socks. Her very manner, even simply the composed way she held herself, seemed more feminine than that of Becca's friends, who all wore jeans and oversized sweaters. "My friends wouldn't have anything in common with her."

Matt noticed that Becca was afraid to meet his glance and warmth returned to his eyes. "She just dresses differently, Becca. You could make her fashionable. Show her the local ways, since you're so good at that."

Becca's face softened. "She *is* pretty. Maybe Mom will take us shopping on the Promenade."

He nodded.

We didn't intrude on the girl's side of the yard, but Matt assembled some of his novels he thought she might like to read, and finally chose a book by Isaac Bashevis Singer because the man wrote about immigrants, and as Teresa was an immigrant he thought she might be able to relate to it. I told Matt I didn't see why she would care about Jews in 1950s New York, but he didn't listen to me. Lately, ever since transferring to Westwind and finding Jewish friends there, he discarded his surfboards and bleached hair and now went to synagogue with them and always spoke about moving to New York. As I myself had followed his lead and bleached my hair and spent my savings on a surfboard, I now felt foolish and was not completely happy about this change. When he told Inay that he wanted to convert to Judaism, she accused him of merely wanting a bar mitzvah with a fancy reception and expensive presents. He persisted, and she asked him what was wrong with him. He asked what was wrong with being Jewish. She said nothing but so long as you live in my house and until you are eighteen you are going to Mass every week. He said that you could not force someone to be Catholic if they did not believe in it, and she said oh yes you could. He said even the priests at St. Dominic's wouldn't have confirmed him if he'd told them he didn't want it, and he only lied to them about believing in Jesus to get confirmed and therefore to please Inay, and now he wished he hadn't. In the end she let him go to synagogue on Saturdays with his girlfriend, Brenda, and her family, as long as he also went to Sunday Mass with us. The Jewish girlfriend's father, Stan Goldman, would come to the house to pick him up, and he seemed to believe Matt's interest in temple was bizarre. He made jokes about Filipino Jews to my mother, who attempted to laugh. Stan Goldman kept asking if all this was okay with our mother, and she said yes. But Matt still had to go to Mass with us and he would sit erectly in the rear pews with a pained look on his face.

He now offered the Jewish book to Teresa after dinner. She looked at him curiously, but thanked him.

"You can read it here in the family room with us," he said. "I mean, if you want to."

"Okay," she said shyly, lowering her head.

Matt and I stayed in the same room, doing our homework, though I kept on the farthest chair from her. She crossed her legs and smoothed her skirt over her pretty knees, and fingered her long hair over one shoulder, then concentrated on the page. Inay kept coming down to the kitchen and making loud irritated noises with glasses and food in the fridge.

At ten o'clock the girl stood and hesitated, as if unsure whether she should address us, and said she was going to sleep. Matt stood. He said he would be interested in hearing what she thought of the book he'd loaned her when she finished, and she agreed. After she left the room my brother paced around a while and went upstairs.

When I later came up to the landing, muffled voices reverberated from my parents' room, and I listened for a long time to their concerned voices before I went to bed.

～✕

The next morning we left for school, but of course the girl did not come with us; no one had had time to register her for classes.

Over the next few days, her mother turned out to be a better maid than Inay expected. Risa woke early, before five, to begin cleaning the

88

house. At first she made breakfast ahead of time and put it in the oven
to keep warm while she did other chores, then took the warm plates
out for us; we had to peel the damp cellophane off the food. The eggs
were dried and oily and the yolks solid and sometimes broken on the
crispy rice. I frowned and Becca complained to Inay. But Risa soon figured out how to prepare the food the way we liked it. She made Father
oatmeal with walnuts and brown sugar, rice and *isda* with tamarind for
our mother. And we found that Risa often fetched us cokes and snacks
without our even asking—even us kids—and she did all this with a cheerful smile. She particularly liked to pamper Father, and treated him like
the man of the castle, bringing his paper to him on the couch along with
a bourbon and ginger ale. It was hard to keep in mind that she'd been
a relative's mistress, because she seemed so devoid of resentment, and
in fact appeared grateful for her place in our house.

Yet though the daughter didn't openly complain, and kept to her corner with her books, she would glance at her mother and disgust came
over her face. She never spoke to Inay. On several occasions when Inay
criticized Risa for some mistake, or sighed impatiently while explaining
some chore, I noticed Teresa angrily walk away. One time she slammed
a door. Risa followed Teresa and told her to be more polite, but Teresa
merely looked at her mother condescendingly, then wordlessly went to
her reading spot in our yard.

Her face showed none of this disgust, however, when my brother returned from soccer practice and found her outside; she liked to sit on a
lawn chair beneath the sycamore tree, sunlight dappling over her calves
and feet. She kept her face in the shade as she read, however, no doubt
so her skin wouldn't get darker. She was pale and tall for a Filipina—
paler even than my own mother, who had much Spanish blood—and
Matt would stand a few feet from her, his hands in his pockets as he
tried to make conversation.

Something about his posture bothered me. My brother had always
been a light-skinned giant to me, but before her his face seemed almost
vulnerable. That his expression would be this way was odd, because
around him she always smiled shyly. Inay sometimes watched them
from the back window, her expression dark and mysterious.

•

From his conversations with Teresa, Matt pieced together her story, that she grew up on our extended family's remote coconut hacienda in a house her father had built for her mother, and he would visit every month from his main home in San Pablo. Teresa liked living near her mother's relatives and had many friends and cousins to play with, but her father's relatives would not speak to her or Risa, for fear of angering his Catholic Church–married wife, and as Teresa grew older it began to bother her. Her father paid for her to go to private boarding school, against his estranged first wife's wishes, and she was more educated (and harder working) than her legitimate cousins, but still shunned.

Her father told her he would send her to private college in Manila, but after he died all the estate went to his first wife, though they had parted many years ago, and the legal Catholic widow refused to pay for Teresa's education. Tito Betino took pity on them, and had them sent over to us.

One day Matt arranged for Teresa to visit his Westwind classes with him. Inay was annoyed, but he claimed that his teacher suggested it as a chance for the other students to "learn something about another country from a guest." Inay, who worshiped schoolteachers, allowed it.

Teresa appeared frightened that morning as Matt drove her off, but when they returned she seemed happy. Apparently she hit it off with Matt's friends at Westwind. At first Teresa had been shocked to learn that nobody knew that the Philippines had been a U.S. colony, though they all knew India once belonged to Britain. She could not believe it. She assumed that a special, benevolent relationship existed between the Filipinos and their former colonizers ("Our older brothers," her *titos* had called the Americans they fought with against the Japanese). She felt like an idiot. There was actually this whole huge country over there that the Americans had fashioned after themselves, where everybody assumed Americans still thought about them. However, Matt's history teacher saw that she looked hurt and he showed an interest in what she had to tell the class, and even acknowledged it was strange that the countries' common history was not in his American history course material, and he promised to add it. A week later, he took Matt aside and asked if Teresa was interested in applying to enter, perhaps on a partial scholarship, and that even midyear something might be able to be arranged.

Matt used to spend a lot of time helping me get ready for bed, and we'd talk as he massaged my legs, which cramped from too much time in the wheelchair, and stretched them to alleviate spasticity so Inay wouldn't have to. My bouts with the wheelchair were less frequent now and I mostly stopped needing his help with stretches, having progressed from wheelchairs to walkers to canes and finally just awkward gait. But the habit of talking continued, and I rarely let him quiet down until past one, and we often got too little sleep.

It was a ritual I loved, but at night now, as we lay in our beds trying to fall asleep, he'd talk about her, even telling me about his intention of bringing her to synagogue. He still attended, though he'd broken up with Brenda. Lately he'd been showing Teresa Los Angeles, driving her to all the same places he used to bring me with his friends, excursions to Venice and Hollywood pool halls and Mar Vista parties that had made me feel older and important. He told me, "Junior, she's a lot smarter than you'd think."

"I wouldn't know," I said. "She's so quiet."

"Her English is actually pretty excellent."

"How? Her mother sure doesn't speak it right."

He paused and even in the darkness I could feel his irritation. Our wall vibrated from Father's noisy bedroom television.

"Well, the girl got sent to a convent school," he said briskly. "Her teachers don't let them speak Tagalog there or teach them anything about their own country. She actually knows more about American history than we do."

You should speak for yourself, I thought, but said, "Why would she want to know about that?"

"It has nothing to do with what they *want* to know, Junior," he said in a newly condescending manner.

I rolled over on my side with my eyes open, and did not say anything; his indignant breathing slowed and deepened and he drifted off to sleep.

One evening a few weeks after her arrival, I saw them in the living room kissing on the couch. I'd come down from our bedroom for a late night glass of water, and heard the low sounds of the television and seen its flickering light coming through the doorless opening to the dining room. I quietly walked into the dark dining room, where I could see them without easily being seen. He had his hands in her hair, and beneath a few pillows that attempted to cover their lower bodies he appeared to be rubbing his crotch against her. The motions appeared rough and ugly. I had never necked with a girl before, nor had I seen my brother doing this, and it surprised me how he rubbed against her like a dog. It bothered me, but I watched for a while before leaving.

The next morning I was working on a model rocket alone at the outdoor table when she sat down near me with a glass of water, a slice of lemon bobbing amid glistening cubes of ice.

"Do you mind if I sit here, Twig?" she said—using the nickname only my brother still used—although she was already seated.

"No."

"Why don't you look at me? You don't need to be afraid. I don't bite."

I blushed and felt angry with her for embarrassing me. But she was smiling at me, like a nice older sister, which made me confused about how to feel about her. She had never, after all, been mean to me personally.

"I know you don't bite."

"Good." She tossed her hair over her shoulder, then fingered it over an ear. "You know, your brother loves you very much."

I shrugged. This was not the sort of comment I answered to.

She laughed, and then asked, "Twig, what is it like to go to your school?"

"It pretty much sucks."

"Don't worry, soon you will make friends. Just give it time, and give people a chance," she said, thus betraying the fact that my brother had told her I was lonely there, something he should never have done.

"I have friends there," I said.

"Yes, of course you do," she said and disappeared into her thoughts, looking across the canyon at the purple woods on its opposite side, then added, "I think I would like to go there someday."

Over the next several weeks, Matt made certain he was around for her to talk to him about her native country. They took walks; they went to Westwood to watch films and amble among the teenaged crowds; he showed her the tourist attractions where our mother usually brought visiting relatives—Disneyland, Universal Studios, Knottsberry Farm. At night he informed me of the fantastic things Teresa told him about the country in which we were born. About dark river-caves you could boat into, filled with blind sparrows that found their way around by chirping, the ceilings lined by red-eyed sleeping bats. About enchanted volcanoes whose springs had procured visions of the Virgin Mary and whose waters cured deformity and disease. About slave ships that had crashed in the nineteenth century and shipwrecked people whose descendants live on some island where they practice a strange mix of voodoo and Catholicism, and how people take boats there from all over the Philippines to obtain cures for their loved ones, and curses for their enemies. About the farm she grew up on, Kawayan, a vast coconut and rice plantation that had been in our family for generations, but which Matt, Becca, and I had never seen; Teresa said its beaches had azure water so clear you could see sunny coral reefs out in the bay. Hundreds, maybe thousands, of poor people lived on the land, living in neofeudal fealty to our relatives.

I had my own enchanting memories. I recalled the sweet dry breezes that blew through the sugarcane stalks on our paternal grandfather's Visayan island. I remembered the magical fiestas, so full of life and family laughing, of dancing for adults who threw coins at our feet, of playing with our cousins at Tia Checerida's beach house, walking over coral reefs in search of starfish and octopi, of learning to climb coconut trees with the houseboys. I recollected a three-month return visit to our cousins' school and what a curious, big deal their friends made of us for being Americans. But in recent years, ever since my brother had entered puberty and began trying to fit in at junior high school, we stopped speaking about returning, and the country seemed to have left our minds.

I had wondered if our mother's disparaging comments about the country ("It's hot, corrupt, and there's a huge difference between the rich and poor") had poisoned my brother's memories. But now I asked myself why if Teresa loved it so much there, she and Risa wanted to live in the U.S., and I suspected she was telling Matt what he wanted to hear. I found his new interest mysterious and disconcerting.

At breakfast one morning, as Father ate the oatmeal Risa had made for him and the rest of us enjoyed poached eggs brushed with hollandaise sauce, Matt turned to Inay and said, "So I didn't realize that the farm in your family was so huge."

"What farm?"

"The hacienda. Kawayan."

She waved her hand and laughed dismissively. "It's nothing. It has no electricity or running water."

"But hundreds of people live on it—on your farm."

"Their grandparents worked for my grandfather, but it took a beating by the Japanese and then coconut prices dropped during the sixties and communists overran it. It's worthless now."

"All those people, though. It sounds like something out of feudal Europe. Like our relatives are some sort of aristocracy over there."

Inay laughed. "We are talking about the Philippines, Matt—that's hardly like owning a piece of Tuscany or southern France."

Matt reddened. "You know, that sounds like something a colonial would say," he said. "To say that a piece of Europe is more important

94

than a piece of the Philippines. Actually, Teresa says the farm is beautiful, that it has mountains and valleys and beaches as blue and as clear
as Hawaii."

"Well, if she wants to live where there's no jobs or electricity or running water, where there's no hospitals so that if you get sick you die—
well, then she can go back. Fine."

Inay took a bite of food, conscious of our quieted table.

"I want to visit," he announced.

"Matt, you wouldn't like the insects, and you're too fussy about your
food. You'd be afraid of germs, just like your father. Besides, it's dangerous. The communist guerrillas would kidnap you."

"People live there and don't get kidnapped."

"They aren't Americans like you."

"Excuse me, but I'm not American."

"You could have fooled me."

He turned a deep, indignant red. "Try telling that to all the white kids
who teased me about being an Asian in elementary school."

"Well, the Marxist guerrillas would certainly think you were American. As long as you look pale enough to have a big bank account." Inay
alone laughed. The rest of us quietly regarded our plates.

"I'm going anyway. And you can't stop me, because I'm *right* about
this," he said, his jaw trembling, then put down his fork and crossed his
arms and looked aside, out the window, at the vines that grew up the
backyard fence like snakes and glittered in the late afternoon sunshine.

Inay observed him across the table. He stood up without finishing
the *bibingka* dessert she had made for him, and he left the room.

A few mornings later, while Matt was at Saturday soccer practice, Inay
asked me to help Teresa bring her bags to the car.

"Why?" I said.

Inay avoided my eyes. "She'll be moving to my cousin Cherry's place
in Torrance."

"But what for?"

"There's not enough room in our house."

"Is Risa going too?"

"No."

"I don't get it."

"They'll spend their weekends together."

"Does Matt know about this?"

"Look. This isn't up to your brother," Inay said crisply. "Now can you please help with the bags?"

The girl was in the living room beside the boxes she had packed, and she stood by the bar, her arms crossed, as I hesitated in the doorway. Behind her, the rear wall consisted of a smoky mirror in which I could see her reflection. She looked stylish—like an advertisement—and deeper in the mirror there stood my own reflection in the doorway, small, brown, and ugly: for all my Americanness, compared to her pale Spanish features I looked like an insignificant little Malay.

"I'm supposed to get your bags," I said.

She turned to me. "What?"

"My mother wants me to help get your bags to the car."

"Then why are you all the way over there in the doorway?"

I tried to hide my blush and crossed the room and picked up a box. It was hardly too heavy for her to handle herself, but she made no move to help. She continued to watch with her arms crossed as I passed her like some houseboy, and then I felt her hand touch my shoulder—only a tap, but enough to stop me and cause my blood to swell in my throat.

"What?" I said in the irritated voice I often used when confronted with pretty females.

"You will miss having me around?" she said, coming closer and touching my bicep in a feminine manner that happened to me so rarely that it roused a confusing heat. I couldn't tell if she was mocking me. Her mysterious eyes seemed sad, but complicated and full of yearning.

"Yeah, sure," I said uncertainly.

Yet before I could say anything more, we heard Inay jiggling her keys in the other room, and my face must have shown my worry, because Teresa's expression grew cold and irritated with me again. I tried to say something, but she brushed past me and walked into the entryway.

In the rearview mirror, I spied Teresa in the backseat. She watched the green streets of our neighborhood disperse, as we drove south toward Torrance, into a bare sprawl of glaring white sidewalks and identical houses. Physically even this was nicer than Manila or San Pablo, but there were no pedestrians, no lively crowds, no colorful jeepneys, no vendor markets, no boys wandering through traffic trying to sell Marlboros and newspapers, no *tsismis* grapevine laughter, no azure skies, no coconut palms and sandy beaches and cheerful yellow Jollibees, only cars and a few Mexicans and deflated-looking teenagers at the dilapidated bus stop benches.

I was surprised at how small the apartment was. Smaller even than our old place, before my father got promoted, and my sister's spoiled classmate called us "third world poor." It had avocado shag carpet and smelled of kitchen grease from the in-room kitchenette, and I could hear the neighbor's television through the thin walls. Inay avoided Cherry's eyes as her cousin greeted first us, then Teresa, and showed us around. The apartment had only one bedroom and Teresa would be sleeping on the couch. Inay's cousin offered us lunch and we ate pork adobo and *arroz caldo* and sweet fried dessert *lumpia* at a small table in the living room; the apartment windows had steamed from her cooking.

Teresa did not look at us when we departed.

On the ride home, Inay kept quiet. The car felt empty. As we entered our new neighborhood's familiar lush streets, she pulled over to the curb and sighed. "That was terrible," she said.

III

Matt came home from Saturday soccer practice with an eager smile and a large book in hand. He'd checked it out from the school library for Teresa, a bulky tome on postwar Jewish immigrants in the Bronx. He looked out at the yard, but she wasn't there, as she normally was before dinner. He sat and began peeling an orange. I avoided his eyes.

"You want some of my orange, Junior?"

97

"No thanks," I said.

Later, when Matt wondered why Teresa wasn't eating dinner with her mother in the kitchen, our parents finally told him that she was gone.

"*What?*" Matt said; he held his fork in the air. "Gone–where?"

"To live with your mother's cousin in Torrance," Father said, in a tone protective of our mother.

"Why'd she go there?"

"There's not enough room in this house for all of us."

"But shouldn't she stay here together with Risa? Risa *is* her mother." He stared at Inay, and she softly fingered her plate's azure and gold leaf edges.

"Look," Father said. "We asked Betino for a housekeeper. We didn't know she was a mistress or a concubine or whatever you want to call what she did. We didn't know she had a teenage daughter coming. That wasn't part of the bargain. That wasn't reasonable, and it wasn't asked of us. But Teresa will be going to school here, getting an American education."

"An American education. A lot of good that does most Americans."

Father frowned. "Seriously, it'll be a great advantage to her."

He tried to adopt a stern and patriarchal tone, one which did not suit him, and Matt ignored it and turned to Inay. He seemed to stare down at the top of her head as she fingered the wineglass before her. Suddenly, she looked so short and dark, next to him, like the mortifying times she'd been mistaken by strangers for our family maid. "Did she want to leave us, Mom?"

She continued looking at her glass. "I will not allow her to get back at me by hurting you."

"Jesus, Mom, are you *kidding* me?"

"I will not have that teenage girl in this house disrupting my family," she said in a cold voice I had not heard from her before. Her tone made my bones contract like a house in winter.

"Jesus, I can't believe you could be so retarded in your thinking," he said.

"Matt!" our father scolded my brother, but Matt ignored him.

"And I asked you a question, Mom. Did she want to leave us?"

Inay crossed her arms and looked aside, refusing to answer him.

"Excuse me, but can you please answer me, Mom? Hello? If you're going to try to self-righteously dictate rules to me and then behave in a certain way, then I think I deserve an answer."

He left the room then, and we heard him thumping up the stairs, slamming shut his bedroom door. He began playing his saxophone, something he knew our parents hated the sound of, and we sat there listening to the grating noise that came muted through the ceiling and vibrated the glass chandelier—and we spoke no more words.

Risa came in to clear the dishes. My father and I avoided her eyes, but when she asked me if I was finished with my coke, I couldn't avoid meeting them. They were huge and wet looking and childlike and I could see how she might have once been pretty and attractive to my mother's uncle. If she was sad, she didn't show it. She smiled at me in her usual cheerful manner, and then at my mother with no sign of resentment.

Later, I noticed Risa bending over plates she was drying, and I thought I saw a glimmer of hurt in her eyes, though of course this could be my faulty memory.

That night, when I came into our room, Matt was on his bed. It was dark and he had the window open—which meant he'd been smoking, something I hated him doing because I did not like to lie to our parents about it, or to get into trouble for keeping quiet.

We lay silently. He did not speak, though he often did on those nights. The open window let in the warm night air, dusty with a eucalyptus scent that emanated from the chaparral canyons around us. A warm wind blew and dry branches clattered gently in the treetops only fifteen feet away.

"You didn't need to be so mean to Inay," I said.

His bed squeaked as he turned to me. "What?" he said, with surprise in his voice at my anger.

"It wasn't her fault."

"Junior, what are you so upset about?" he said, sounding bewildered and somewhat amused as he came over in the near dark and tried to place a hand on my shoulder. I shrugged it off. "Don't touch me."

He recoiled, holding his hands up as if he had touched a hot stove, then regarded me for a long moment. "Junior, you don't know anything, do you?" he said.

"You're the mean person. You made Inay feel bad."

I heard him sit back on his squeaky bed and sigh. "So, does this mean you're not going to hang out with me and ask my advice on things anymore?" He sounded more resigned now than angry, and waited for an answer. But I gave none.

"She's the daughter of Mom's uncle's mistress," he finally said.

"So? That doesn't mean Inay should have to take care of them."

"You know, he could very well have forced himself on Risa. He might have *raped* her, Twig."

"That's still not Inay's fault."

He paused and studied me again, for a long moment this time. "Don't you get who that girl is?"

I hesitated.

"It should be obvious, Twig."

Wind gusted. Our window rattled. Somewhere down the street an empty rubber trashcan fell over and rolled about on the gravelly asphalt.

"She's Inay's first cousin."

He leaned back against his headboard again, and though it was dark, I could see by the moonlight that he was waiting for a response—some kind of grunted shock, or realization—but, getting none, shook his head and looked outside at the moonlit clouds that crept over the eastern horizon.

For some reason those last words failed to make much of an impact on me that night, though I remember them well now. Over the following days Matt refused to speak to our parents, except in critical tones—finding fault with Father's new country club and career as an administrator, accusing our mother of vanity in the obsessiveness with which she applied her makeup and the fastidiousness by which she avoided the sunlight so as to keep her skin from getting more dark. He called her colonialized, a snob, ignorant. She never berated him back, only defended herself meekly, but when he was out at night, my father still at work, I found her crying in the dark living room, lights off. My brother continued to drive to Torrance to see the daughter. He met her after she got out of classes, because Cherry felt uncomfortable letting them see each other knowing how our mother felt about this. But Inay knew what he was up to, and they argued over it loudly enough for me to hear them through the walls. One time I was in the family room as Risa was ironing clothes and watching TV with me, when we could hear Matt shouting at Inay about what a terrible person Inay was. Risa didn't meet my eyes.

Nothing my mother said, no matter how angry or heartfelt or humiliated or tearful or pleading, stopped him from going down to Torrance. I decided it was up to me to protect her.

On Monday, a day Matt and I usually rode our bikes to hapkido together, I purposely left before he returned home from soccer practice. No doubt he must have waited around for me, because he came into the dojo late, having to bow before the instructor and ask humbly for permission to enter the class. His forehead touched the sweaty blue mat. Then he raised his face. With the instructor watching, he did not dare catch my eye in the workout mirror. Master Lee Cho III grunted at him, then made him do fifty push-ups in front of everyone, causing my brother's face to go red. Our master then let Matt find his humiliating place at the rear of the studio with the white belts who were several ranks below him. During the sparring sessions, I avoided being paired up with my brother, and would not meet his glance.

Afterward, I hurried to my bicycle, despite the fact that doing so made my limp more awkward, my gait more jutted to the side; my fingers had trouble unlocking the rusty chain that ran through the wheel spokes. Matt caught up with me.

"Why aren't you looking at me, Junior?" he said, stopping several yards away.

101

"I'm busy unlocking the chain." My fingers jittered on the links as I pulled them through the spokes. He glanced aside, at the departing cars and the gregarious students so happy to be in their street clothes again, then turned back to me.

"I missed you earlier."

"I'd left already."

"I noticed that," he said. I did not say anything more, and he added, "Look. I'll buy you a sundae. My treat."

"You know, she was talking about you the other day."

A change came over my brother's face and he seemed suddenly aware of the other students around us, in earshot, walking to their cars. "Who?"

"Teresa."

"What did she say?"

"She was laughing at you. She said you had a crush on her, but she didn't like the way you walk all awkwardly and nervous, and that she thought you were creepy the way you always looked at her with big puppy-dog eyes. But she put up with you because she felt sorry for you and had nothing better to do. She said she couldn't understand why you kept on giving her books written by Jews, and she could tell your Jewish high school friends laugh at you behind your back for going to synagogue."

I gripped my handlebars, intending to pedal off immediately, but my shoe slipped off the pedal onto the sidewalk, the aluminum teeth cutting into my ankle. He started forward, wanting to help, but stopped himself. Recovering, I could not avoid my brother's eyes: his face was crumpled with hurt. I finally managed to bike away, cutting tire marks in the yellow pollen, the sun warm on my face as it poked through the overhead branches and flickered, stinging my eyes.

Later I would, of course, spar with him again. He quietly made sure new students knew to augment their fighting style to accommodate me, despite their lower belt, but tried harder to make sure I didn't notice. He held himself back from shielding me from stares in public, sensing that I no longer wanted him too. But Matt was not one to hold grudges. He still had my back at school, as I would find out later. And we would have conversations in the dark when we should have been sleeping. But they were never the same as they had been—whether this was mostly due to him or me, I do not know—and he soon left for college. Perhaps this is the nature of things between siblings as they get older, and what happened with Risa and her daughter was only incidental. But after he was gone I could not help thinking about how I had acted and the way he looked at me, and how all this happened so soon before he left for Amherst, without proper time to make amends. It seemed strange, and still does now, that we can be so close to someone, for so long, then become apart. We live in separate cities now and though for a time we did not speak much to each other, we now do annual ski trips with our families. It is often a merry occasion, and our children play well together. But we never talk about Risa and her daughter.

IV

She actually did go to high school in Torrance where she received an American education. She did not do well in my mother's cousin's home, that small one-bedroom apartment in a cheap complex with fake grass in the courtyard. I heard about her "wildness," the drinking, the drugs, the pregnancy, her many white boyfriends and a black one, and how she dropped out of school. The times she came to pick up Risa, she sat in the running car, honking but refusing to come inside. Her mother would hurry out, signaling for her to be quiet, and the daughter seemed to have disgust on her face as she stared forward and as she drove them away. A year after her pregnancy she moved to San Francisco with some boyfriend, and her mother—whom we had grown to love having around—sadly left us (she cried as she hugged each one of us, and especially Matt), to live closer to her granddaughter.

For several years Inay tried to convince Risa to return, and Risa, who had always fondly pampered my father, would think about it but finally say she could not leave the city her daughter and grandchild lived in. In any case, after my father lost his administrative job due to office politics, they had less living space and could not have paid Risa what she deserved. I think Inay only continued to ask her to return, because Father had taken the humiliation of his job loss hard, and she was working hard to lift his spirits and believed Risa would help. We received a few postcards from the area—Daly City, Milpitas, Hercules, Vallejo—then they tapered off. Somehow Risa and her daughter seemed to have vanished into the vast diaspora of Filipinos who lived up there but whom, for some reason, nobody ever seemed to notice. We heard fragments of biography about them, some contradictory, that Risa had taken up with a widower boxer she nursed while working in a hospital, that Teresa had taken up with another guy—a black man—but none of these were substantiated and I do not know where they live or what became of them.

New Relations

I was too young to get married, even at twenty-eight, and possibly that also explains why I invited my mother to meet my new wife's family, a week after the wedding, without warning her to be prepared. We flew back to California from Tahiti, where the ceremony took place, and Inay smiled politely as Carolyn gave her a videotape of the service. My mother wore a slightly nervous smile in my new wife's presence, as she nodded at Carolyn's vivacious laughs, and tried not to stare at her blond hair and blue eyes. Later, I noticed Inay glancing at my wife's back. As we watched the video of the ceremony she did not make any negative comments about the conch blower, or the Polynesian female minister who wore a seashell necklace around her fleshy neck and looked like she should be weaving baskets to sell to tourists, and Inay did not express any negativity when Carolyn mentioned to her—in anxiously reassuring tones—that the woman was an actual Methodist minister. Carolyn had no idea that to my mother, a product of Philippine Catholic schools, this was hardly a reassuring statement, as none would have been, short of telling her that this minister was actually, contrary to appearances, a male Catholic priest.

In the hallway before bedtime, I ran into Inay on the dark stairway, and she hesitated before setting her hand on the railing and turning to me.

"How do you like her?" I said.

"She seems very nice."

"She *seems* very nice?"

"I just met her, Matt. But she does seem lively and self-assured."

Inay glanced aside, cupping her elbow—which is what she did when nervous—as the street lamp glowed through the window and caught her nightdress like moonlight. Outside, giant eucalyptus trees rustled invisibly, like sand in an hourglass, the air thick with their pungent scent.

"She comes from a real good family," I said. "New England and Lake Forest, Chicago. Her father went to Duke and *Oxford*."

Inay had often said with pride that people back in Manila knew the names of all the Ivies better than most Americans did in Los Angeles—or parts of the Midwest, where my American father came from.

"And Carolyn's grandfather went to Dartmouth," I added.

Inay nodded, without enthusiasm. She should have been sore at my impetuous act of running off and getting married, outside the church, without a word or invitation to the family, before I had even finished my schooling and gotten settled in a career. But she didn't seem sore—or angry—and this puzzled me. After she retired to her bedroom, I stood in the hallway a long moment and tried to figure out how I felt about it. We'd all be traveling to Chicago to meet my wife's parents the next day (minus my father, who was visiting his cancer-stricken sister in Vancouver), and I wanted to be prepared.

My childhood bed would feel odd to be in with my new wife, and as she brushed her teeth in my old bathroom, I lay on the bedspread and looked around. On the walls hung the same old pictures I'd chosen ten years ago, some embarrassing: a photograph of a surfer in Bali, a cornice jumping skier, a silly pastel watercolor of a pool and palm trees which I'd never have chosen after taking art history in college. Even worse, my mother had framed and hung a few of my own junior high school drawings, acrylics, charcoal etchings that earned praise from my teacher Ms. Fernandez but which made me redden to look at now, and which I couldn't believe were on display for all my parents' guests to see. It was like a guestroom at a B&B where the theme was "Matt's room, decor ten years ago, teenage faze." She'd replaced the single beds my brother and I slept on with a queen-sized mattress and oak headboard, and put a fancy matching oak chest at its foot, and a

French country-style writing desk by the window. I would have loved to possess furniture like this when I actually lived here. Most of my junk had been cleared from the shelves, except for whatever knickknacks I'd acquired over the years that Inay thought looked nice: a wooden carabao from the Philippines, several sets of bookends, a falsely antiqued tobacco-colored globe. On the bookshelves were textbooks and classics from high school, some critical editions from college, but also several mass-market romance novels my mother or her guests must have put there. Bodice rippers. Harlequin. I began collecting these for the trash pail, along with several issues of *Cosmo* and *Self*, so her visitors wouldn't think they were mine.

Carolyn came out and watched me. "What are you *doing*?"

"Throwing out these stupid books my mother put on my shelves," I said.

"Those aren't yours?"

"*No* they aren't mine. I think she must've put them here for her guests."

"Well, it's her room now, so maybe you'd better leave them."

"But everyone will think I own them, since this room's ostensibly mine. I seem to be the theme."

"Matt, you're twenty-eight years old."

"So?"

"Don't you think you're a bit old to be worrying about what your mother does with her own home?"

"Well, then she should get these stupid pictures I drew in high school off the wall, and eliminate any pretense this room is mine anymore."

Carolyn looked at me skeptically, probably imagining that I'd feel offended if my mother actually did this. She began to walk about the room, looking at the pictures now, as if in a gallery, timidly touching the framed glass and smiling.

"What?"

"You drew these?"

"I was young."

My wife came over and put her fingers in my hair and smiled. "You're still young, Sweetheart."

107

We did not make love that night because the new oak headboard lay against the same wall my parents' bed touched on the other side. I lay awake as my new wife grew hot beside me—she always did when sleeping—and seeped her warm scent into my old pillowcases. Carolyn was a graphic designer at an Oakland firm; up until now I lived only a car-crowded bridge away, in a loft on Portrero Hill, and worked at a law firm in San Francisco's downtown financial district, near the Embarcadero. We met only seven months before, on an alumni trip to Turkey led by Oxford scholars: she had gone to Middlebury and I to Boalt Hall, and for some reason these universities mixed up their alumni on this same trip. The brochures had sounded promising, a chance to see ruins with actual archeologists, rather than the typical American tour group abroad, but we found that we were among the youngest on this trip of fussy, silver-haired retirees, and were inevitably paired off: being both different than our older co-travelers, and from the Bay Area, we seemed to have the world in common.

Now as we lay in bed, I thought about my mother's odd manner out in the hallway. Had something been missing? Yes. She hadn't nagged me the way she used to. All my memories of childhood and high school are flavored with the nagging voices of Filipina relatives—*titas* and *lolas* and Inay—telling me to come inside so I wouldn't get "too dark," to eat more so I would not be so skinny, to not spend time on extracurriculars but to study so I could become a doctor and make the family proud. She tried to tell me what friends I could hang out with (nerdy ones who studied), and when I brought home my grad-school Mexican girlfriend, Lucinda, Inay acted cold toward her. Lucinda belonged to a Latino pride organization and spoke during dinner about the need for bilingual education, and my mother finally said that if her people did not like America why didn't they go back to Mexico; it was the same sort of thing she told her own relatives if anybody complained about the American bases at Subic Bay, or how Americans colonialized Filipinos by forcing on them their language—she'd say, *Ay nako. If the Philippines is so great, go back.* And yet she would watch the Manila news program on cable and religiously keep up on Pinoy events. She fretted over elections there, cried at the images of people killed or injured by the volcanic eruption of Mount Pinatubo, involved herself in family gossip from thousands of miles away, sought out the Filipino markets clear across Los Angeles. Sometimes she made fun of Filipinos–how poor they were, the carousing and mistress system, called them *lazies*–but other times she complained about Becca and I turning out like spoiled Americans who felt no reverence for old people or any faith in God, though she left out our disabled brother Twig. She often reminisced sadly about how many nursing homes there were here, as opposed to Manila, where supposedly none were needed. Her vacillating attitude toward her native country, a place of which I only had fond memories mostly regarding fatty food and easy friends and doting relatives, made my siblings and me confused.

After dinner I told Inay, in private, that she'd been rude. She told me that Lucinda was a bad match for me–her mother was divorced, hadn't even baptized her daughter, and had children from three different fathers. I asked her what that had to do with Lucinda, and my mother said that a person picks up traits from their family, that when two young people marry, their families are joined too, and so I had to listen to Inay–with her age and experience–when she told me that Lucinda was not the girl for me. I told her that this was not the Philippines and people did things differently here, that families did not marry, people did, and mothers did not pick their children's spouses ("And besides, you're just being snobby. Don't think I haven't noticed how our relatives in the Philippines look down on poor people. It's a totally elitist, unfair system and you're just being colonialized." "Colonialized? *Ay nako makulit na makulit k'ayo!* What are you talking about?" "Trying to climb and stay on top, like the Spanish." "Excuse me, so I am not allowed to point out that your girlfriend has bad traits just because she grew up in the ghetto?"). My graduate studies weren't going too well at that time–I was frustrated and unhappy with all the contentiousness– and perhaps the stress explains why I yelled at my mother before I returned to my apartment early. In the end Lucinda left me for another man–maybe my mother had been right about her–but I stopped talking to Inay about my girlfriends, and she did not meet Carolyn until after we already tied the knot.

The crisp air of late autumn greeted us as we stepped off the plane; across the runway, foliage blazed with sunbathed color. Carolyn had been particularly cheerful the flight over, ordering three glasses of wine for herself and one for my mother, who normally didn't drink on flights but took it with a nervous smile. For some time her expression puzzled me—this grimace she made in front of Carolyn—and as we waited for our bags to spit out onto the conveyor belt, I noticed the way Inay twisted her purse strap in her manicured fingers. But it wasn't until we stepped outside and looked for my in-laws' car, that I realized—as Inay glanced at her reflection in the glass—that she was nervous.

My new in-laws' red Audi pulled up to the curb; a few fallen leaves lay on the hood, and the wipers had caught a few pieces against the glass. Carolyn's father, Elliot, remained behind the wheel, a preppy-looking man with silver hair and high cheekbones, but my wife's mother stepped out and held her arms open to Carolyn. She was very beautiful and tall and my wife had to tiptoe on her high heels as she hugged her.

Then my mother-in-law looked over my wife's slender shoulder at us and you could see she had been told about my mother being Filipino by the way she did not at all look surprised.

Inay relaxed a little at seeing her warm expression, and approached.

Carolyn's mother—Lynn—was apparently a take-charge woman, and managed the deft introductions, putting both myself and my mother at ease through compliments and small talk. She wore a simpler dress than Inay—who'd brought her fur coat (a hand-me-down gift from her *tita*) despite my insistence that nobody wore those anymore outside of Vail and Texas—and Lynn lacked my mother's oversized diamond ring and earrings received from rich aunties before leaving for America thirty years ago, and which she seemed to have brought out for today's occasion.

Seeing these at breakfast that morning, I'd fought an impulse to tell Inay to take them off, thinking I was too old to concern myself with my parents' behavior. Now I tried not to look at them.

"It's so nice to meet you, *finally*, Matt," my wife's mother said, holding my shoulders and looking at me as she smiled and shook her head, then cast a playfully rebuking glance at Carolyn; my wife was in the Audi chattering away with her father; he waved at us and mouthed *hi* through the windshield. They didn't seem overly upset at the fact that we'd just eloped.

Lynn turned to my mother. "And you too, Dina. Carolyn's told us all about you."

My mother's fingers gripped into my arm. "Oh she has?"

"Yes."

"And I've heard about you, too."

Inay was a bad liar and as she spoke a tense smile framed her teeth, oddly white against her brown skin because she'd obviously had them whitened, but fortunately Lynn had glanced back toward Carolyn.

Then Lynn focused on my mother again. "I thought we'd go up to the house, Dina—so you can settle in—and then we could maybe hop over to the village where they have boutiquey shops where we could look around."

"Certainly," my mother said, in an excessively formal manner.

My mother used to take my sister and me on drives through poor areas of town to warn us what our lives would be like if we didn't study hard. She took us to places our white father wouldn't dare enter, or our classmates either, to Compton and Watts and South Central and East LA, to neighborhoods where the sidewalks were warped and cracked and the sun glared off—unshaded by any trees—and weeds grew out of the battered streets. When Inay first came to America, she lived and worked in the Crenshaw district and similar neighborhoods, which had bigger Asian populations then, and went into the projects where she made friends with the black people who protected her during the sixties Watts riots, hiding her on the backseat floor as they drove through angry crowds—so she was not afraid of these places. She took us past schoolyards where the black teenagers congregated around basketball courts and smaller black kids stood in the intersections trying to sell us weed, boys who walked right up to our car and knocked on the glass. My sister sat petrified beside me, staring forward and avoiding their eyes, but refusing to let our mother on to the fact that we were scared.

"So how would you like to live here, young lady?" Inay said to her.

Becca shrugged in mock indifference. "I wouldn't be afraid."

"If you don't study hard this is where you could end up."

"Oh, please, Mom."

"You don't believe me."

"I think there's alternatives between being a doctor and living in Watts," Becca said.

"Not everyone has the advantages you and your rich friends at your private school have had, young lady. You must remember that."

My sister, who wanted to study acting at a conservatory of performing arts, rolled her eyes. "This isn't the Philippines," she said. "And if you didn't want me to be around rich kids then you should've let me go to public school like I wanted to."

Becca hated it whenever our mother brought up being poor in the Philippines, and would say that Inay had no right to wear such poverty like a badge of honor, since she had come from a once-wealthy family, and had lived better than most Filipinos even in her final years there. (In later years, Becca and I would learn about how truly bad it had been—how the Japanese had burned down their houses, destroyed crops, executed relatives. How her mother Camille had received an urgent note of warning from a Japanese officer friend one night, explaining that they were to be executed the next day. They had all hiked in the jungle dark—whispering—down to a beach, then took canoe-like boats by moonlight. They had been so deadly quiet Inay could hear the oars on the water, the breathing of the rowing men. We would learn how Inay's family wandered through villages pillaged by Japanese in retreat, past bodies of children and women and men bayoneted to save ammunition. A fetus in the dirt.

But back then we did not believe a woman with her attitude could be anything other than sheltered.)

Inay said it had been humiliating to have to live off relatives—with this memory of money—worse than if she'd been born poor, since poverty of pride is worse than poverty of money, as evidenced by the poor people in the provinces being so happy; that claim infuriated my sister, who would shake her head and turn away.

"You American kids believe that money will grow on trees for you," Inay said. "But just you remember that being an artist will not pay rent in *Brentwood*. Just because you are not a black person does not mean you won't end up being poor."

"I know plenty of artists who don't live in the ghetto, Mom."

"I bet their parents give them money, or these girls live with older men."

"Jesus, Mom, you are so paranoid."

But apart from nagging us about our studies, Inay pretty much couldn't help indulging us in every way. During our early childhood years she didn't work, but devoted herself to our happiness—she took us to the beach to swim or to Crestwood Park for hiking every summer day, and when I got old enough to go surfing she bought me a board and took me to Malibu three times a week. She brought us to family parties where we ate *lumpia* and "chocolate meat" and tamarind *isda* and sweet rice *bibingka*, and when we got old enough to want only American food that is what she made us. In those late childhood years we tried to nag her into going back to work—all our friends' mothers had. We worried that she did not have a life, and of course we envied our friends who came home to empty houses without nagging Moms (these were the years of latchkey kids, when most children were allowed to roam around unattended). But Inay worried too much about perverted kidnappers and neighborhood injuries and bad-influence friends to leave us unsupervised. And she wanted to be around to enjoy our company. And she wanted to keep vigilant watch over our gestating dreams—to make sure they were prudent and respectable, fixated on things like business and medicine and science. Most of the other Filipino mothers we knew—relatives and family friends—were the same way, and we would gather with our cousins and Flip friends to complain about our clueless mothers.

Lake Forest, in the northern suburbs of Chicago, is a lot like a small New England town, with bucolic hills not typical of this normally flat region; it had a cute village center of stone-faced buildings with restaurants and cafés and boutiques. We drove through residential streets that burned with autumnal color. It was the tail end of an Indian summer and you could still smell the dead leaf dust in the air, and dust got all over our fingers and clothes and the windshield and hood; it covered my polished shoes when I stepped out at the old gas station to stretch. Inay kept looking around curiously at the vegetation she'd never seen before. Back in California the air was too dry to hold bucolic smells, whereas here the foliage scent seemed to swim around you. Nor do I think Inay had seen such houses—Queen Annes topped by looming turrets and cornices, Arts and Crafts homes crowned by heavy drooping eaves, sagging screen porches, estates fronted by leaded windows revealing library alcoves.

"It's an old house, Dina, let me warn you," Lynn said to my mother. "I know you Californians are used to conveniences."

"I like old houses," I said.

"Oh yes. They have very much *character*," Inay said with a forced formality, using one of my sister's favorite terms, one used on our vacations up to my godmother's place in San Francisco where the old Victorians on her street had been renovated and painted cheerful pastel colors.

Carolyn's father laughed. "*Character!*" he said, slapping his leather steering wheel as if Inay had made a great joke. Elliot, who attended English boarding school, had the manner of someone used to being around people with a dry sense of banter, though none of us were particularly participating now.

"The house isn't much," he added, waving his hand dismissively. "The rooms are tiny, made when people were small from being malnourished, and the floors creak and the windows are small. You'd think people didn't like light back then. But the place is in Lynn's family so we keep the *old thing*."

The "old thing" was a large three-story house fronted by a metal plaque indicating its historic landmark status, and it was tucked onto four wooded acres they owned, sandwiched by a stone former Episcopal church and a French Colonial–style mansion; it had been in the family since the late 1800s. Somehow he let it slip out that one of his wife's ancestors had fought in the American Revolution. It was an English Tudor house with a jumble of sloping roofs, from various add-ons over the decades, including a wing drafted by Howard Van Doren Shaw, on the highest of which was a copper weathercock that had gone green. Behind it a lawn sloped down to a stream and trout pond over which a wooden footbridge led to an incongruously placed tennis court.

Inay stared at this thing—this makeshift mansion—very quietly, and Lynn took Carolyn aside and asked if my mother was feeling all right or did she possibly need an Advil, but I knew my mother was only trying to hide her awe as they led us around the grounds.

The inside, however, was dark and the rooms small, and their kitchen had been remodeled during the 1970s to let more light in, so everyone had to eat at a long bench that was less than formal. In fact, you had to admit that nowadays nobody would have built this house as it was, that it was no wonder they spent most of their time in a renovated Back Bay brownstone, where Elliot worked as a banker in Boston, and kept this one as a mere vacation house, like a family pendant you hid in a safety deposit box and passed down over the years. There were even some hippyish touches left over from the 1970s and New Age 1980s (Lynn had apparently been a bit of a free spirit back then), which hadn't been replaced: a rosewood sculpture of an arching whale, a Santa Fe–style watercolor of an adobe hut fronted by a buffalo skull, and a pink Native American feather. Several objects suggested a former Asian religious fetish: various Tibetan throw pillows, a framed mandala with French lettering of a Parisian museum beneath, a Zen gong. More recent additions seemed to come from India, brass joss stick holders and silky pillows in a reading nook possibly used to meditate. Inay seemed to relax, and even began to engage my new in-laws with stories about Los Angeles and the O.J. Simpson trial—especially interesting them with the fact that his family used to attend our Catholic church, one of his kids went to the same school as Becca, and I used to live in an apartment two buildings down from his murdered wife on Bundy Drive. She didn't mention that we were scholarship students, or that the only reason we'd been able to afford to live in Brentwood was due to my father's promotion to assistant principal at another school—a job he lost after three short years.

"And Carolyn tells me you're from the Philippines?" Lynn finally inquired.

Inay hesitated. "Yes."

"That's so *nice*! Such a lovely country!"

"You've been there?" Inay said with surprise, and stiffened beside me.

She would have been happiest if no Americans ever traveled to our native country to witness its embarrassing condition. At home, she always pointed out that she had lived in America more years than the Philippines, and long ago became an U.S. citizen. She announced that Filipinos had not always been such illiterate and silly people, that when she left during the 1960s it was the second richest country in Asia and had the region's highest literacy rate, and classes were taught in English as they had been when it was still an American colony. She often took great pains to emphasize the fact that not all Filipinos were poor and uneducated—an impression the rest of the world only got because poor people were the ones who had to leave to find work. Among her American friends, she made too frequent references to her great-granduncle—Jose Rizal—who was a poet, novelist, *European trained* surgeon, and the Philippine national martyr. And that her brother's alma mater—Santo Tomas—was *older than Harvard*. In the company of Filipinos she derided the fact that most of the Filipinos you saw abroad were the poorest ones—the domestic laborers and bar girls and agricultural workers—and that our greatest visibility was through the news coverage of mail-order brides and maids who'd been whipped by their Singaporean and Taiwanese and Saudi Arabian employers as if Filipinos were lower than dogs.

"I've only been to the airport," Lynn said. "In Manila, on our way over to Singapore. Elliot had business there."

Lynn glanced over at her husband, who was peeling pistachios from a shell and not paying much attention.

Inay relaxed a bit, recrossing her legs. "Well, Manila is a bit crowded for me. I would not suggest it for a vacation."

Elliot looked up. "Oh, we don't vacation, we *travel*. Like those folks in that Berto-what's-his-name movie with John Malkovich. You know, where they're out with the Arabs in the desert. We'd be more interested in the local customs and such anyway. Now that we have relatives there maybe we'll go back for a *real* visit."

"Sure," Inay said, looking alarmed.

"I heard the family unit is real strong over there, not like the mess we've got ourselves into over here in America," Elliot said, sadly shaking his head.

"I like Americans."

"Oh sure, Dina, I know you do. But let me tell you, we even have a Filipino girl in the family now and I've seen those family values in action."

"A Filipino girl in the family?"

"Sure. A nice girl, married my younger brother, Carolyn's Uncle Rob. He found her through the mail, or something."

"I see."

Elliot turned to my wife, and Carolyn shifted uncomfortably beside me. "You probably know more about that than I do, don't you Carolyn?" he said.

"I think Mia comes from Mindanao," my wife said, looking at her knees and smoothing her skirt flat.

Her father turned to my mother and said, "Do you know Mindanao?"

She tried to smile politely.

"Not very well," she said. "It's in the south of the country—*very far* from where I was raised. They are almost a *different people*, really. A different race. They speak different languages and are Muslims."

"Oh, no. Mia's *Catholic*—just like you. Or was, anyway. She converted to the Protestant faith when she married Rob."

Elliot began to inform us of their courtship and her virtues as a wife. "She's completely devoted. Doesn't complain, not like so many people around here do," he said, giving his wife a little ironic glance, which received a challenging look in return. "And the crap she puts up with with Robert—let me tell you, my brother's no piece of easygoing *cake*, I am ashamed to say."

"Oh please," Lynn said.

He ate another forkful, and continued, "At first, I have to admit, Lynn and I, maybe even the whole family, were a bit skeptical about the whole thing. You know, why would she want to marry a stranger she doesn't even know, will have to even *sleep* with the guy, she must only be wanting a U.S. citizenship, et cetera. Well, as it turns out it wasn't actually like that. There was a real courtship and everything. Robert found Mia's ad in some magazine and he wrote back to her and they arranged for him to fly over to the Philippines—a long flight, as you know—and he met the family, spent some time there, completely chaperoned by the brothers and parents, nothing illicit about it at all. After a month of this he flew home, then wrote to her parents to ask for permission to marry her, for the daughter's hand, so to speak—real old-fashioned . . ." (Elliot turned to Carolyn) ". . . not like these young American kids do, just going off and getting engaged and even *married* without so much as a thought to their parents' wishes . . ." (he appeared amused at Carolyn's refusal to look at him, and turned back to my mother, whose face wore an increasingly difficult smile) ". . . and Mia's parents said *yes*, and Robert flew over a month later and they married and he took her home to America."

My father-in-law pushed his plate away, laughed at his own story, and shook his head.

"They have two twin daughters, been married for five years now," he said. "You should see the way Mia takes care of Robert, sponge bathes him and everything. No. It's the real thing. A genuine *sacrament.* She really did want to marry him."

Now that Elliot had finished, the table was quiet save for the clanking of silverware and the sipping of soup. There seemed to be a need to break it up, and Carolyn's mother turned to mine.

"Dina, you'll *love* meeting Mia. You two will have so much to talk about."

"Oh, yes, of course," my mother said with her forced smile.

My mother unpacked a houseguest present for Carolyn's parents, and Lynn took it ("Oh you didn't have to do that!") and tore off the gift wrap, revealing a blue Ming vase. Inay explained that it was imported from Manila, apparently not realizing that this meant it was a cheap Philippine knockoff of something Chinese, but then she explained that it had belonged to her dead father, and was a family item.

Lynn and Elliot looked surprised, then awed and honored as it occurred to them that they were indeed family now—with this stranger who apparently took this in-law thing *very* seriously—even though they lived across a vast country and would likely rarely, if ever, see each other again. Lynn put some yellow lilies into the blue vase, arranging them elegantly and setting them on the inlaid bedside table of Carolyn's room, where they glowed beautifully before the antique leaded window that looked over sunny poplar trees.

"I know you don't want to meet Mia," I said to Inay in the attic-scented alcove where we had retired to rest. We sat on twin wing chairs, meant for reading, the leather upholstery split to reveal yellowed foam innards that irritated my neck, and we faced windows that looked over the pond and small flagstone chapel folly owned by my new in-laws. The trees were bathed in amber sunlight that angled in through the branches.

"Why wouldn't I?"

"I don't know. You seemed a bit awkward about it when her parents brought it up."

"That's not true." Inay hesitated. "I just hope they don't have any wrong impressions."

"Well, if you don't want to go, we don't have to. I'll make up some kind of an excuse."

"I told you I don't mind meeting her."

"You don't mind—or you *want* to."

She paused. "I want to, Matt."

I turned to look out the leaded window, across the lawn my wife had played on as a girl. The liquid glass gave the outdoors a look of myopic aquatint. "Are you having a good trip?" I said.

"Yes, of course."

That night a cold front came over Chicago off the western plains and we could hear our window rattle and the walls contracting around us, the metal radiator pinging. Outside a soft snow fell about the nimbused lamps like glowing halos, and cars sloshed on the street.

"This is a great house your parents have," I said.

Carolyn had her comforter up to her cheeks, peering at me, and she shrugged beneath them. "I guess so," she said. "We never lived here full time, so it doesn't feel like my home. I don't have a room here the way you do at your parents' house, anyway. Not that I would want one. I think it's unhealthy for a grown kid to stay with their parents at home."

"Well, but on vacation."

"Still."

I lay on my back looking at the ceiling. Back in Manila my cousins all lived at home until they married, and even after that. It seemed to me that in most of the world people lived three generations to a household, an arrangement that worked out fine. You did not have nursing homes in Asia, or childcare by strangers either. And most people in the world didn't have the *luxury* of individual rooms. I, of course, had been very American, left home for an East Coast college three thousand miles away, then chose to work in distant cities like London and Miami. However, I eventually got homesick and returned to Los Angeles for grad school (in philosophy, which I would abandon as an A.B.D. to pursue a law degree), no longer an adolescent pushing for independence; I moved into an apartment near my parents' place and ate over there a lot. My girlfriend at the time and I had had arguments about this—while at grad school she thought I shouldn't be taking my parents' money, and she was relieved when I finished.

"What?" my wife said.

"I didn't say anything."

"I can tell you want to. What are you thinking about?"

"Nothing," I said.

"Okay."

"It's just that, maybe it would've been nice if you'd told me about this plan to visit your uncle and his Filipino wife this weekend."

"Why would it matter?"

"No reason, except, you know, with my mother here and everything."

"It won't be too crowded."

"I know, but still."

"Well, they invited us to see *both* of you. You *and* your mother."

"They told you this?"

"Well, no—but I'm sure Mia wanted to meet your mother, since they both come from the same country and everything."

"I wouldn't be so sure," I said.

"What do you mean?"

"Not all Filipinos are necessarily dying to meet each other."

Carolyn hesitated. "I'd have thought your mother would've wanted to meet Mia. I thought it was pretty nice of my parents to set a meeting up this way. In fact, I was sort of surprised at how your mother responded when my father said Mia was from Mindanao."

"Surprised at how she responded," I said.

"Never mind."

"No, how were you surprised?"

"She just seemed strange about it. Well. That's just how I felt when I saw her. Like she wasn't enthusiastic or something."

"Mindanao is a long way from Manila," I said. "It's like a different country."

And though this was true, it was not the whole truth I had in mind, though I did not bring this up to my new wife on this occasion.

Carolyn's Uncle Robert lived outside a small town in rural Illinois. It was as if we drove into winter. The temperature dropped thirty degrees last night. The wind here blew hard, and the land was so flat it seemed the wind must have flattened it. Autumn's leaves had already been stripped and flung away. We drove past open farms, a few nearly naked trees that stood skeletal in the distance, once in a while a gully with woods, and traversed little bridges we would slow over for fear of ice. The dead harvest lay broken on the soil, like old bones, and snow from last night kicked up in sheets and blew over the fields, dissipating like frigid blown-breath.

Carolyn leaned over the back of her father's seat. "How can they live way out here, Dad?"

He shrugged. "It's cheap."

"But it's so depressing."

"*Mia* doesn't seem to mind," he said.

Each time my new father-in-law spoke the mail-order bride's name, which was often, a somewhat wistful tone came to his voice, pregnant with approval and hidden meaning. Sometimes I couldn't figure out whether he was teasing his wife and daughter, or trying to convey approval to my mother.

My mother betrayed no reaction. She had spoken about Filipinos from Mindanao before, at home, after having a few sips of her favorite cocktail, a Mai Tai, among relatives, a little frown and a tipsy word or two about those *dark Muslims from the south*. She and my *titas* and *lolas* decried the embarrassing existence of mail-order brides, which they saw on *Donahue* with fat white soldiers and truck drivers and losers, who made white people think all Filipino women were desperate for American men.

"I'd have thought the poor girl would have missed the warm, tropical weather they have over there in her native country," Lynn said.

"Mia's not a complainer," Elliot said.

This was Amish country and we passed old, weathered houses that had no antenna or phone lines; stiff, dark laundry flapped from wooden clothespins. As we drove by several horse-drawn black buggies, Inay stared incredulously at the grim bonneted women and stoic bearded men who drove them.

Carolyn's Uncle Robert was a professor of South Asian Studies at a local state college, and though he was seventeen years younger than Carolyn's father, he had already been married twice before—once to a girl from Thailand, and a second time to a Vietnamese girl. He believed that Westerners in developed countries had lost their family value systems, which is why he liked to live among the Amish, whose families tended to build houses next to their parents'—the reason you saw clusters of adjacent farm homes on single plots of land. All this Carolyn told me. I didn't ask her why Robert, if he believed so much in family unity, had moved away from his parents' city, or left his parents' religion, the Episcopal Church, and belonged to an evangelical one now.

You could see Robert and Mia's house all the way from the highway, across several acres of barren field, and we approached on their long dirt drive. We found Robert in the open garage working on his Suburban, and he wasn't the loser I expected him to be—but a red-bearded, muscular young man in wire glasses that gave him a look of handsome intelligence. My mother regarded him curiously, and I couldn't help feeling she was contrasting him to my father, who certainly married a Filipina from a higher-class family, but who'd grown into a humiliated, sometimes dispirited man who rarely left his home. Dad had met her while in Palawan working as a teacher and trying to gather stats for his PhD, though he never finished his dissertation. He weathered this first defeat, and several others, taking a job as a public schoolteacher in LA, proudly housing Inay's mother and brother in a cramped apartment, and hosting her constant stream of visiting relatives from Manila while he slaved away toward a promotion to administration, which he finally achieved for a time. He bought us a house tailored to provide a nice living space for his wife's mother and brother. Yet only three years later, his well-earned job was taken away from him due to office politics in a publicly humiliating fashion. They'd had to sell their house at a loss, and move back into cramped quarters, which seemed smaller now, disheartening. And though Inay tried to bolster his confidence with her tenderness, his humiliation seemed to have a permanent effect.

I thought Robert's attention would go straight to my mother, but he greeted us men first—with firm handshakes—before focusing a smile on her. "Nice to meet you, Dina," he said. "I've heard all about you."

His attention embarrassed Inay, who made her own greetings with an involuntary bow of her head and eyes, oddly girlish, and we went inside to find Mia.

She was in the kitchen, hovering about the stove. She was a tiny, dark little woman who moved about with a peasant's manner, and revealed crooked teeth when we greeted. However, she wore a handsome Ann Taylor double-breasted suit—no doubt for our sakes—with a trim silk yellow scarf knotted at her neck, and had an expensive haircut that complemented her features. Yet her expensive makeup could not hide her sun-damaged face. She was still beautiful, though. She'd been hard at work on the food, while attending to her two girls on nearby high chairs, and greeted Carolyn's family and me warmly, though she seemed ashamed—I noticed—to meet my mother's eyes.

Mia finished feeding her kids first, and then moved them off to another room, to keep the dinner table safe for adult conversation. We ate from steaming dishes full of *pancit* and *lumpia* and tamarind fish soup and other native dishes that I had always loved but rarely had at home because Dad didn't like them—he preferred meat and potatoes—but which Robert and my wife's family dug into and complimented.

Often during the evening, I felt Mia regarding me, but when I met her eyes I did not understand what she wanted.

Mia seemed to be a quiet person but she played hostess, inquiring from her in-laws about our drive down, and our sleep last night. Then she fell quiet.

After a time, Robert turned to my mother.

"So it's a real amazing coincidence how much we have in common in this family now," he said.

"Oh yes." Inay held her fork in the air, nodding at him.

"I heard your husband has a PhD, too. And from Chicago."

"He did attend Chicago, but he doesn't have a PhD."

"Oh—" Robert hesitated. "But he does have a master's."

"Yes," my mother said. "All but dissertation."

She spooned a piece of adobo pork onto her bed of white rice, and took a careful bite.

"And where in the Philippines do you come from, Dina?" Robert said.

"Luzon and Visayas."

"Mia comes from Mindanao."

My mother glanced at Mia, who concentrated on her plate, eyes lowered, then my mother turned back to him. "I see," she said.

A silence passed.

"Do you go back often, Dina?"

"No. Perhaps a few times since I came to the States twenty-seven years ago."

"Oh, that's a shame. Mia and I try to go back as much as we can—

four times now since we got married eight years ago. I love it there. I think the way people live over there with their families and eating and laughing a lot is wonderful. A real cheerful people. But I suppose I can understand why you might not go back much. It's a real poor country," Robert said and shook his head, turning to Carolyn's father in explanation: "They live in nipa huts made with thatched roofing, Elliot, and when the typhoons came last winter Mia's family's house blew down. They don't have electricity, medical care, nothing. The literacy rate has gone to shit ever since they had to deal with that American-pawn dictator Marcos."

Robert shook his head and turned back to Inay, giving her a sympathetic smile. "So I can see Dina, why maybe it isn't nice for you to go back, to have to see all that."

Inay's lips hardened, but she kept her mouth shut and continued to eat.

"This adobo stuff, this chicken dish? It's great," Elliot said, eating merrily. "Do you have to cook it on a wood-burning oven, to be authentic, like at the Pizza Kitchen?"

"Actually you just use a stove," Inay said.

"I noticed, Robert, that you're handy with cars," I interrupted. "Did you build that tree house, too?" I pointed out the kitchen window to the backyard, where a well-built structure perched on an oak tree bough, though it was actually supported by stilts.

"Sure did," Robert said, smiling. "I also built the nursery up in the attic."

He began proudly relating his carpentry skills, *authentic* methods he had learned by studying the Amish. His recounting of the admirable, if frugal, ways of those Anabaptists somehow led him back to his pontifications about the poverty of the Philippines, apparently a favorite subject. It was horrible. He seemed to have the idea that every ill there was due to the American colonial occupation, something my mother would no doubt disagree with—for three of her guerrilla uncles would have been executed by the Japanese if MacArthur—a man she worshiped—hadn't returned. The Japanese had executed an aunt. She witnessed a pregnant girl get her stomach ripped open by a bayonet, the fetus

125

tossed into the air, then caught like a shish kabob on the way down. Her brother Pepe still groaned at night in his cot in their mother's tiny back bedroom from memories of guerrilla fighting. Robert began rehashing about two hundred thousand Filipinos dying at the hands of American soldiers in 1902, mostly women and children starving in concentration camps, speaking to Elliot but clearly for my mother's ears, though she looked irritated and gulped down her glass of wine. Robert told Lynn and Elliot a story about his last trip there, and how he saw Smokey Mountain, an enormous garbage pile visible from the azure Manila Bay, in which *twenty thousand* poor people lived so they could scavenge for scraps of food. The babies mostly died, and the ones who lived had such strong immune systems they could spend the rest of their lives living in the caverns and mineshafts dug into the side of the trash mountain among the rotting food and excrement all dripping and baking and steaming under the hot and humid sun.

Lynn and Elliot looked horrified.

Robert shook his head and turned to my mother. "So I really can see, Dina, why you haven't returned much. Maybe it isn't as nice for you to visit, to have to see all that again."

My mother sat stiffly. "Actually, our family had electricity and running water. I just do not see a reason for going back. I am an American now," she said sharply, glanced at Mia, then concentrated on her food again.

I kept still in my seat. There was something odd about the way Inay had said this—and it seemed to come across differently than intended.

Mia lowered her head, and Robert's fingers stilled on his silverware. My face burned. He seemed about to say something, but held his tongue.

From the way Inay concentrated on her food, I sensed that she'd had too much to drink, and couldn't get her mind off what was eating at her. She shook her head as she ate, frowning, then sipped her wine, and added, "My family actually had quite a modern life."

"Yes, we know that Mom," I broke in. "Mia, can I have some more *lumpia?*"

"Yes, of course Matt."

The woman hurried to pass the plate to me. The egg rolls smelled rich and warm on their damp bed of napkins.

"Matt, I was saying something," my mother said, regarding me harshly.

"Okay, Mom. I didn't realize."

Her gaze remained on me. "You kids have always interrupted me," she tried to whisper, though everybody could hear.

"Mom. Please. I wasn't doing that," I said, blushing, and reached for her wineglass—lipstick smudged the rim like clinging rose-petals—but she held it away from me.

"I'm not a child, Matt. I can drink wine if I want."

She turned to Carolyn's parents—who appeared mortified but politely smiled at her—and said, "In fact, we all went to private—*Catholic*—schools. My brother's university is older than Harvard."

"That's very impressive, Dina," Lynn said.

"How about some salad," I said.

"Sure," Elliot said quickly, and passed it over.

My mother reached for the wine bottle, and everyone watched her refill her glass.

She told us stories about the country she came from, the archipelago in which I had been born. They were untrue mostly, though not always. She spoke as if she had forgotten she was in the company of Americans. She told us how her brother lived in Forbes Park, a walled neighborhood that was separated from the dirty and unsafe areas of Manila around it; how his alma matter, Santo Tomas University, was older than Harvard; how most of the Filipinas she knew, or was related to, were educated in American or European universities and were doctors and engineers and businesswomen, not nannies and maids and go-go dancers. It was the same sort of talk that was so amusing when done by my gossipy *titas* and cousins in Manila, or in our house, even enchanting. But now, as I looked at the tablecloth, I could barely hear the timbre of my mother's voice, for the tightness of my breath and commotion of my heart.

Robert clanked down his fork and stared at her, half rising.

"Mia is not a maid or a go-go dancer," he said.

127

"She never said I was," Mia said, rising with horror and touching her husband's arm.

He shrugged her hand off, glared at her for interrupting, then glowered at Inay again. She looked afraid now—his red nostrils were flaring and his fists clenched—yet he hesitated, as he noticed my mother's vulnerable eyes, and seemed to have forgotten what exactly she'd said to offend him so much. He swayed a bit. Suddenly, she looked very small beside him, tiny and brown.

"Robert, sit *down*," Lynn said coldly, and he obediently did. His face turned the color of a Christmas ribbon as we all ate in silence.

Afterward Mia served *leche* flan and *bibinka* dessert, coming around behind us and refusing to let anyone serve themselves—even my mother—and then Mia checked on the kids in the family room. Then we went to see the nursery and the blue walls and ceiling she'd painted for the baby. A sky of white clouds, and a mountain topped by Noah's Ark with its gentle, pale patriarch and his cheerful animals. Robert did all the talking, while Mia cupped her hands before her. Inay made some pointed praise about the painting; she seemed more sober now. As we all moved through the hallway, she glanced at me with worried, remorseful eyes, but I turned away. We walked outside and toured Robert's yard, the frozen playground set he'd constructed and the dormant vegetable garden he said Mia planted, and then it was time to depart for the long ride back to Chicago.

Parting at the doorway, I noticed Mia reach out to squeeze my mother's elbow, and something exchanged between their eyes.

Mia and Robert waved from the driveway with the halfling children beside their mother, as she hugged them protectively from the cold and shifting wind that blew in from the western plains.

In Lake Forest, I lay on the bed with a book and waited for my wife to finish her bathroom routine so I could brush my teeth, and by the noise she made as she moved about—the clattering of toiletries and banging of cabinets—I sensed she was irritated. She sat on the bed, but avoided my eyes and turned on her lamp and took up a book.

"What you reading?" I said in a conciliatory tone.

"Nothing."

"Okay, what did I do wrong?"

"Did I say you did anything wrong?"

"Well then, why aren't you looking at me?"

She sighed and set her book on her knees, then set her hands on the cover and turned to me. "I guess I was just a little surprised at how your mother seemed around Mia."

My pulse quickened and I stilled my own hands on the bedsheet lump my thighs made from beneath. "I'm not exactly sure what you mean."

"Look. Maybe I shouldn't say anything."

"Actually, now that you've started I'd kind of like to know what you mean."

"You promise not to get mad at me?"

"Sure."

"Well, I thought your mother was sort of rude. Look, don't stare at me like that. It's partially your fault too, you could have at least stopped her or told her to be more polite. And don't try telling me she wasn't. At first I wasn't sure—your mother just seemed quiet, and so I thought maybe she was being shy, though you'd have thought she'd be excited to meet someone from her own country. I mean, when I was a student abroad in Paris all the Americans were all over each other and felt like we had so much in common—you'd have thought we'd all came from the same little town, not all over the country. But I thought—maybe Matt's mother is just shy or Filipinos are just quiet around new people they meet, or it's because they're around all these white people and feel self-conscious. But then at dinner that remark your mother made about her own family having electricity growing up—and the way it made Mia grimace and look down at her plate. God, I felt so sorry for Mia. I know your mother and Mia come from the same country with their own class baggage and everything, but Mia *is* my family. She *is* an in-law, and I have the right to be offended. So don't look at me all indignant like that. Your mother is so prejudiced with her stereotypes about maid-order brides. Mia's this sweet girl who can't help the fact that she was poor and without electricity on some little island your mother's people don't like, and just because your mother is a minority doesn't mean she can't also be a snob."

Carolyn hesitated, realizing she had worked herself up, and now avoided my eyes. She cupped her hands on her lap, and appeared remorseful as she looked at them.

"Thank you for informing me so well about what a terrible person my mother is," I said. My voice came out constricted because my throat and chest felt so tight.

Carolyn looked up and I was surprised to see that her face was contorted and she said, "Oh, please. Don't try to bend this around to distract from the way Mia was treated today. I have a right to be offended. In fact, I think somebody owes Mia an apology."

"An apology."

"Yes, from your mother."

"You're kidding."

"Of course I'm not."

"Look, she can get a little talkative when she drinks too much wine. But Robert and—" I said, then stopped.

"What?"

"Never mind."

"No, what did Uncle Robert say that was so horrible? You can't say because you can't even remember his words you think are so bad."

"I think we should stop this conversation."

"So you're still saying that you think your mother treated Mia fairly tonight?"

"No. What I'm saying is—I'm saying that I don't think either of us should be saying anything right now."

"Oh, that's great. That's really productive. Just let things fester. That's a real mature way of dealing with solving a relationship problem, one which, by the way, your condescending mother started by . . ."

Her face had become oddly contorted and strange to me as she spoke, in a manner I never noticed on her before, and it didn't change until after I stood and paced and pressed my fingers into my temples and then finally aimed my fist at her parents' antique leaded window. I managed to veer it away at the last moment, however, and my knuckles slammed into my grandfather's fake vase instead. He had died when my mother was young and I never knew him. It smashed against the wallpaper and porcelain pieces fell onto the carpet. My hand came away torn and I felt warm dripping beneath my pajama sleeve.

My wife looked shocked and then the hatred was gone from her face and she looked pretty again, and she came up and wrapped my hand in a towel ("Why did you do that to yourself? You stupid, stupid, silly boy."), and held me.

"I'm sorry, Sweetie."

"Well, that's okay," I said. But I stared forward and did not look at her.

I worried over the scuffed wallpaper, as if it was more important than my mother's place in her new family. Porcelain pieces lay on the carpet among the fallen wet lilies. My grandfather's vase had only been a cheap imitation of something foreign anyway, I told myself. It must not be worth mourning over.

My wife touched my earlobe. Her fingers felt puffy, larger than when we first met, though she was only three months pregnant now. "Will you forgive me?" she said.

"You know, your whole family might be nice and polite to Mia, but they treat her differently than they would an American woman. I'm not necessarily saying a lot worse, or even any worse. But it's different. I think maybe my mother senses that and she just doesn't want to be treated that way."

"Of course, Sweetie, I'm sure you're right," my wife said, burrowing her face into my chest. She had apologized, but it came out so fast I was not certain she'd really listened to what I'd said. My words seemed inadequate anyway. After a time I realized she was crying and so I sighed and stroked her hair and told her it would be all right. We'd had fights before in our short relationship, but they always ended with us forgiving each other and saying we were sorry and making teary love, so that it all seemed like it was just meant to bring us closer. We always forgot what we'd said. But as I sat there staring at the ceiling, at an ugly painted water pipe, I could not empty my mind.

•

There is a gesture my mother made the next day that is strange now for me to think of. At the airport we parked and saw my mother to the gate. I passed her the carry-on bag I'd hauled up to this point, and handed over her ticket. Carolyn gave her a hug first and when it came my turn I had to lean over and was surprised at how small my mother's body was—that she was such a little person. When we drew apart her eyes avoided mine. She instead sought out Carolyn and offered an odd smile. If this had been my mother's native country, my new wife and I might have moved into my parents' home, for a year at least, a cost-saving ritual perhaps also designed to introduce the bride into her groom's family dynamics, since they would someday be taking care of his parents. Maybe it was even a way to let her know who was boss. However, Inay had not chosen to stay in that country, but to become an American, and today, as she paused before the gate, she offered my new wife a strange smile I had not seen on her before—it seemed eager to be warm, even to please—and then she turned to board her plane.

Winter Dog

The boy came up to her and asked what she was doing. Nancy stiffened, caught off guard because she had not realized that anybody was observing her as she wandered, back and forth, among the twilight streets. The boy looked at her oddly and she realized that she was wearing her thin blue nightgown, which flapped coldly about her skinny legs in the frigid December air. She could not imagine how she hadn't noticed how inappropriate this was when she came outside.

"I'm looking for a dog," she said.

"What kind?"

"A black poodle. Have you seen a black poodle?"

"Maybe. I think I might have seen one over on the other side of Lincoln Park."

"Could you show me?"

He hesitated. "Do you drive?"

"We can walk."

"It's a long way in the cold. Especially if you're not dressed right for it."

"I'll be warm from walking."

The boy—who couldn't have been more than eleven—studied her warily. He held a red bike, though he was not on it, but kept it alongside him as if walking it across some street. The wind caused the bell to produce a faint continuous ring.

"I don't know if I should. It's a long way in the cold and it's windy. Snow's even blowing in off the cornfields."

Indeed in the enormous flat park behind him soft sheets of snow blew in off the cornfields—remnants from last night's gentle dusting—and rippled over the frozen lawns, among dead trees, like softly audible drifting sand.

Nancy frowned, angrily.

"I think I can make my own decisions, thank you. I was probably scolding my sons when your mother was a little girl."

Nancy's voice sounded irritated, but the boy's sweet eyes looked scared—no doubt he was worried about being rebuked by his own mother, the poor thing—and she felt sudden remorse. She added, more softly, "Please, young man. It's my son's dog. I've got to find him. It's cold outside. He's not an outdoor dog. I was feeding the stray cats on the porch and he must have gotten out without my seeing it."

"It's your son's dog?"

"Yes, he lives in Los Angeles. His children go to high school with celebrities. They're very intelligent—scholarship students."

"Why do you have the dog then?"

"He gave it to me without asking. One day his whole family showed up and gave it to me. A pain that dog has been. Totally undisciplined, it pees on everything, leaves poop on the carpet, smells up the whole house and leaves hair on my furniture and bed. But it's the thought that counts. They probably thought I was lonely, and needed company, so they bought this dog without asking. Brought it on the plane. It's a real nuisance and is probably better off dead. But if my son and grandchildren find out the dog's lost and died, because I couldn't see it go out the door, they'll get their feelings hurt and maybe worry about me."

She sighed as they walked. The cool wind billowed her nightgown against her legs, icy air seeping in like needles.

The sky had turned from orange to red and purple, the leftover clouds from yesterday's storm still ablaze and moving like rapid brushfire. Yet the street gravel she walked on was getting dark, making her squint, and the houses' living room curtains flickered with blue television light. Probably nobody was going to notice her now, which was a relief, since in her nightgown somebody might come out and accost her.

"What's more, Seth will accuse me of being blind or absentminded, unable to take care of myself," she continued. "And those kids will be so sad thinking of that lost puppy."

The boy nodded. "I've got a dog myself."

A smile came across Nancy's face, which seemed to provoke a joyous feeling in her body, accompanied by a memory of Seth playing with his pet lab—what was its name?—back when he was still young and skinny and took it with him bird hunting out at the lake by route 76 among the grass and weeds and he would come back most days without a catch but not discouraged nonetheless, his face reddish—which Nancy sprayed with Solarcaine, provoking a cute scrunching frown; and on those days he did return with a fowl, his face looked so proud, and the dog seemed to pick up on Seth's excitement and slapped its tail against his jeans, muddying the warped kitchen floor, as it circled about, barking and panting.

Nancy said to the boy, "What kind of a dog do you have?"

"A black lab."

The same one as Seth's—what was the name?—amazing! Then she recalled some of the messes, the chewed laundry baskets, torn-up flowerbeds, the paw prints on the kitchen floor, the duck feathers and blood stains on pillowcases she had to wash. "I hope you clean up after it yourself. I hope your poor mother doesn't do all the work."

"No, I do it."

"Well that's good."

"Are you sure you're not getting too cold?"

"No. I'll tell you if I do."

She forced herself not to hug herself, now that she'd said this, although her nightgown fabric was cold and stiff against her arms and shoulders.

The boy seemed to be thinking, brows furrowed; something bothered him. Nancy wondered what it was, but did not want to pester him. The thoughts—and worries—of children could be mysteriously unimportant, though intense. For them the death of a pet could rattle as deeply as the death of a husband or child. Nancy was only coming to understand this now.

Finally he said, "Why don't you move out to Los Angeles, if you're lonely."

Nancy smiled.

"That's what you've been worrying over just now?"

He seemed embarrassed and shrugged.

"No, there's no way I would live in the same house as my son and daughter-in-law—Dina's her name."

"Why not?" he said. "Is she mean?"

"No. Definitely not. My son would never let anyone be mean to me. I'm not saying that."

"No. No. Of course not."

"Let's be clear about that."

"Okay."

She studied him, stopped now; satisfied, she continued walking.

"In fact, she's suggested I move in with them, many times. But I always refuse. Those people out there don't know how to live or be kind to each other."

"I wish I could move out there."

"You do?"

"Sure. It's boring here. And I hate the winters. My Dad says he wants to move to Austin, Texas, where it's sunnier and interesting, but we're stuck here because my grandma's getting old and won't move too."

"That's a pity," Nancy said.

He walked silently, and then added, "I'd go out there if I were you."

"Well, I see what you're saying, but the thing is, young man, my son's mother-in-law has lived with them for twenty years. She's not there anymore now—went back to the Philippines, that little poor country in Asia where she's from. Which was a good thing, because she was a strain on my son's finances. I, for myself, would never impose myself on them—to be such a burden."

The boy watched her intently now. He had grown really quiet, and Nancy figured he was shy.

"You're a quiet type, aren't you?"

"Maybe," he said, and then suddenly said, "I'm sure he'd be happy to have you live with him, from what you've said."

136

"I know."

"Are you not going there because you're afraid . . ."

"Well, for years I've been telling Seth that it hasn't been right to have Camille living off him, with him being a young man with a family and everything. Not with Camille having her own rich son in her native country, in the Philippines."

"She has a rich son there? I thought you said it was a poor country."

"It is. But in those third world countries, they have rich people there who live off the backs of the poor people. It's not like America there. No middle class. Anyway, his wife, Dina—my daughter-in-law—found out that I was saying that they shouldn't have to support her mother. She knows I've been saying it for years. Pestering my son. And she's been real nice about it too, still invites me to live with them. Even now after he lost his nice job, and they had to move back into a little apartment. And I think she means it too. But there's certainly no way I could live with them now—I mean, even if I had wanted to. Of course, I don't need to. Fortunately, I have my late husband's house. He was always proud of being independent, and I agree with him too. I'm quite all right on my own."

Suddenly, she saw a shape moving, ahead in a thicket of bushes—small, quick, the size of a little dog, the gait of something frightened—and she hurried forward, calling out "Baby!" the name of her son's dog. The shape receded into the thicket's darkness. She hurried faster. The frozen grass on which they walked crushed under their feet, and she slipped on a patch of solid mud beneath the embedded strands; her ankle turned and she reached out to grab the boy as she collapsed onto one knee.

She stopped falling then—thank God—with only the one knee having made contact with the cold ground, a hard shock that nonetheless rattled throughout her skeletal frame. Yet she still clung to his jacket, a fistful of quilted down in her hand, surprisingly little to get a hold of, and when she looked up she saw his horrified face.

"Are you okay!"

"Don't worry. I'm fine." She quickly pulled herself up; her bony knee throbbed where it hit a patch of icy snow. Her nightgown clung to the wet skin—maybe her knee blood, maybe melted snow.

"I think we should get back now," the boy said.

"But my son's dog," she said. "Don't you care about that puppy out there alone in the cold? It must be so worried!"

He followed her to the thicket. But they found nothing—it was either scared off, or wind had fooled her by blowing branches.

Snow had begun piling on the boy's blue hat, accumulating in its woolen wrinkles, and she noticed now how beautiful, and pale, was his face—with its soft freckles and long lashes and reddish snow-dusted brows. The fear in his face touched her: a fear not of her, but of consequences. She had to pull herself together for his sake. The cold was confusing her thoughts.

"Listen, are you old enough to drive a car?"

"No."

"Do you live nearby?"

"Well, sort of—across the southern part of the park," he said. "Why?"

The southern part of the park—how far was that? The park was large, cornfields and random woods and creeks up until Enid Yodder died three years ago, and now a confusing mass of woods and lakes and paths and grassy expanses on the northern edge of town.

"Maybe we can go there and your father and mother could drive us."

He hesitated.

"Can't we go back to your house?" he said.

"You don't want to bother your Mom and Dad?" she said.

"No," he said, then glanced at her scraped knee and thin flapping nightgown. Nancy realized he was worried about bringing a shivering old woman into the house, in a nightgown; that his parents would no doubt be furious with him for bringing her across the neighborhood in the snowy cold. How could she have been so thoughtless? The cold was affecting her brain, she needed to warm up her thoughts to focus on the task at hand, before it was too late—she imagined finding the dog with its stiff fur alone in some snowbank, the teeth and bluish gums exposed, how horrified her grandchildren would be to find out.

"I'll wait outside and you get the keys," she said.

"What for?"

"We'll heat up the car. Warm up. And you can get me a coat I can borrow."

With snow on his bangs and lashes, he looked at her reluctantly, seeming not to know what to do, and obediently nodded. Suddenly, as they walked again, she noticed he had a limp, and realized that he reminded her—oh so much—of her disabled grandson, Twig. The sweet one. It was this boy's kind countenance too, his thoughtful eyes, full of worry, beneath thick bangs that fell over his pale forehead, like eaves, and the faint traces of freckles half-hidden by his red parka collar that cradled his slender neck.

The house, lit from within, had windows that glowed warmly like eyes; it was still early enough that they had not yet closed their curtains, but late enough so that you could see into the house: the family sat in the living room, facing the blue flicker of a TV.

She saw the boy enter and discuss something with the father. Nancy worried that the boy would ask him for the car key—against her instructions—but he did not, apparently, because the father made no objection, and soon the boy was coming down the front steps, with fitful skips, and signaled for her to come to the car.

It was a huge Lincoln, and by the time she reached it the boy had already gotten into the driver's seat and started the car. She sat on the frozen cloth seats, and the heater blew still cold air on her body, which seeped through her silky nightgown, the soft fabric tugging at her goose bumps.

The boy observed her.

"You're shivering."

He held a black wool coat on his lap, yet for some reason hesitated to offer it to her—why shyness, of course!—until she asked him, and he passed it over to her with a blush.

The wool was warm with the warmth of his house, and full of kitchen smells (cinnamon, orange, and something else), as she wrapped herself in it.

"Thank you so much," she said to the boy. "We'll just stay here until I can warm up a minute, then look for my son's puppy."

"Okay."

The air began to warm as it blew around her arms and ankles, sifting her nightgown like a flag, and to fill the car with a pleasant smell of damp musty wool. She leaned her smiling face toward the warm vent and closed her eyes—it felt like desert air off the Mojave sands on that drive she took up to Mammoth Mountain with Seth's family that time, when she stepped out of his car at a gas station and was surprised to discover that a night wind could blow so dry and hot, filled with the distant rumble of semitrucks, the scent of rock and sand.

When she looked at the boy again, he was observing her.

"Warmed up yet, young man?" she said.

"Sure."

"Okay, let's go look for my puppy."

"It's too cold out. I don't think we should."

"But my son's dog!" she said, her heart racing again. "What if it's got into that huge park? It could get *lost* in there."

"Please, if you caught a cold, I might get in trouble."

She thought this over. She wondered if the boy was also worried about walking with his limp, which maybe got worse in the cold, but was too embarrassed to bring it up. After all, Twig's limp got more pronounced by day's end, and also in extremes of temperature. How she missed Twig! Or maybe this boy had overprotective parents.

"Okay, I'll drive."

He hesitated but she persisted and he finally let her scoot into the driver's seat. He sat beside her, and as she pulled out onto the street, he glanced nervously about. She promised to keep to the park roads and rarely used side streets, though he did not look reassured. She felt bad for him and inched along through the park. It had no lamps, and the car's headlights seemed to cast a lone orb on a canvas of blackness. Pretty soon she lost track of where in the park they were. If Seth's puppy were out there wandering about on the frozen grass, she would not see it unless it was caught in the beams, so she swerved back and forth.

"I'm only swerving like this so we can see Baby," she said. "Don't worry. I'm not drunk."

"Its name is Baby?"

"I can't remember its name. Seth's son, Twig, named it. So I just call it Baby."

As the night drew a thick span of stars overhead, the illuminated blue water tower rose above the cornfield tops to the west—near the gravesite where Ned lay buried.

"It's nice that your son's family gave you that dog," the boy said. "They must miss you."

"I suppose so," Nancy said.

"Maybe his wife wouldn't mind it if you went there—to Los Angeles."

She turned to him. "I thought I told you, I *know* she doesn't mind," she said crisply.

The boy hung his head, and she realized she'd overreacted. She berated herself—bit her knuckle as punishment—and parked the car so she could turn to him safely. She kept the heater running.

"I'm sorry I snapped at you," she said.

"That's okay."

"No it isn't. I don't know what's got into me." She sighed. He looked so rebuked, his voice having shivered, and she longed to explain.

"Let me tell you a story, young man. My late husband came from an ex-Amish family. Now I have a great deal of respect for the Amish faith—but one thing they tend to do is to emphasize community over the individual. They're almost Catholic in that regard. That's why you see so many of their houses around here built corner to corner—the grown children build theirs on their parents' farm, touching. My husband's sisters had to play with dolls without faces, because faces were too individualistic. Well, there are some advantages to community life—especially when it comes to raising children, not being lonely and such. And people nowadays talk about the Amish like they got some wonderful lost way of living. But it's overrated, I can tell you. We moved in with Ned's parents right after we married, and your business was everybody else's. His mother was constantly judging me—and everyone else. Nothing was good enough. That's why they left the Amish—the Amish weren't good enough for them. And of course the Amish thought my husband's family wasn't good enough for them either.

141

"I had a hard second birth—that's my boy Seth, the gentle one—he was inside backward and with his leg cramped up, by the time the midwife had him turned around and out, I was worn, sick and tired. I lay in bed for two months. Like a wet rag. I never knew skin could be sodden before. I had a fever and would look up from my dreams and see my boy in the arms of my husband's mother. During that time she looked after my boy. Which was a help, of course, but she got too attached; I'd awaken and see him in her arms with those faceless dolls. When I got well enough to pluck those sticky sheets off me and to get out of bed and I wanted to take over, she resisted. Held him against her chest and told me I needed to keep in bed. She said I needed more rest. When I refused the rest, and plucked him back and into my arms, she hovered about me and little Seth—all the time. He'd come out too early, skinny and weak, and I knew he needed . . .

"Anyway, I told my husband that his mother was hovering, and he told me I was imagining things, being too hard, she'd gotten attached to Seth, et cetera, is all. Well, okay I thought. Maybe I am being too hard.

"Then it came time to baptize little Seth. He was already getting older than most babies were when they got baptized in my church—the Methodist religion, which was different then than now. Well, my mother-in-law had a fit and said it was wrong to baptize an infant—*apostasy*, I think she called it. I refused to budge, and for the next week my mother-in-law bore on me with chores and criticisms about the way I was raising my son and then on the morning of Seth's scheduled baptism I woke up and found that my baby had been taken to my mother-in-law's sister for the day. She claimed she'd forgot. My husband came into the bathroom and found me crying there, alone, by the sink.

"He took me and Seth away from his mother, and refused to speak to them since. It was hard—we had little money of our own, since he'd worked on the family farm. It was the Great Depression and he labored for less than a dollar a day. Farms. Construction. Factories in Decatur. We moved about from town to town, all over central and southern Illinois and into Indiana, out to Nebraska, wherever he could find work. Eventually he preferred to work on his own—ran taverns, pool halls, fixed up houses we lived in and moved on. For two years we lived in a hardware store behind a sheet and used the paint tub sink to clean ourselves, and the children showered after gym class at school. My husband didn't let anybody tell him, or us, how to live, or how to raise our children.

"I tried to get him to make up with his mother, but he wouldn't, not over the next thirty years—he stood up for me. That touched me. It was sad that he didn't even go to her funeral. But he did it for me—to make a point. My husband was a difficult, cantankerous, irreligious, independent man. But I stayed by him until the end, and he is a man I most admire."

Nancy ran out of words and emerged from the space of telling and remembering to this car, warm and moist and steaming windows, with the boy in it; he looked at her with a distracted, worried expression, and she forgot how exactly she got to this point in her story, and where she was going with it, and why.

"Where are we?" she said, gripped by a sudden worry.

"I don't know. Somewhere in the p-p-park."

This boy stutters. My God, what have I done to him?

"Where in the park?" Looking around it was so dark and she never came here at night and everything looked unfamiliar.

Their headlights lit a space out of the blackness before them. Snow blew now fiercely, in rapid gusts, and a white sheet of it moved over the grass before them like an upraised sail, illuminated in the headlights, with an illusion of being unmoving.

A small animal emerged into the twin beams. "Baby!" she blurted out, suddenly remembering as she saw the little dog scampering within the sheet of light. "My boy's puppy!"

"What? Where?" the boy said.

"There! Ahead!" she pointed.

But he did not appear to notice this puppy, which even now was receding into the vast darkness outside the illumination.

"I don't see it."

"Why, it's lost!" she said. "It's lonely! But it's afraid of us.

"It doesn't know . . ." she started to add, as she slammed down on the accelerator so the headlights could catch it. But she had not noticed

143

that the field on which the puppy stood was actually a frozen lake, and the tires slipped beneath them for a moment, rippling over the protruding reeds she'd thought were stalks of long grass, as the boy screamed and touched her, and then she could feel—as if she were a part of the car itself—the ice breaking beneath them, the coldness within, opening to embrace this kind boy's father's warm and generous car, and the people inside.

Family Friend

One day at the park in Rustic Canyon, Tomas was frying burgers while his biological son sat on the boy's mother's lap. She had an arm wrapped around the boy's chest from behind, because Em suffered from weak muscle tone and had difficulty keeping upright. She laughed at something Tomas said, and the boy fell off her knee and hit his head on the concrete barbeque pit.

Em looked up at her with fear and confusion, as if for an indication of whether this hurt was bad enough to warrant crying. He saw the look on Veronica's face and started sobbing. She held him up at the armpits as if he were a baby and not nearly forty pounds. His legs dangled like a rag doll, feet flopping against the ground. "*Shhh*. It'll be all right. Stop crying. We're in public, people can hear you. Don't scream. Come on, Em. It wasn't so bad. Tomas? He won't stop crying. Tomas, can you check him? I don't see anything like blood. Why won't he stop crying? Please Em. Please."

Then she leaned to Tomas, whispered: "He feels hot. Does his skin feel hot to you? Oh God."

He carried Em like a little toddler, his little shoe tips dragging against the park dirt, while she took the clattering walker. The boy's face felt feverish against Tomas's cheeks. Slippery with sweat. As they reached the truck, Tomas was sweating where he pressed against the boy's hot clothes. The boy did not stop sobbing.

As Tomas drove to the urgent care center, he was aware of his body perspiring beneath his shirt, as if he were on his way to do a performance. He was rattled by his heated son crying beside him, but there seemed—troublingly—to be something else too. He sometimes acted in stage plays, as a sort of hobby, and it discomfited him to realize that he was acutely aware of Veronica's eyes studying him driving, as a casting director scrutinizes an auditioning actor. When she had become pregnant with the boy, six years ago, and told him it belonged to Tomas, not her estranged husband, he had asked her to divorce the man and move in. They would raise the boy together. She had considered it; but he was an aspiring actor at the time, financially unstable, and she decided that for the sake of the boy she and her husband should raise it; he reluctantly agreed. She asked him to keep his biological status as the boy's biological father a secret—for the sake of the boy—and promised that he would get to see him regularly as a beloved family friend. "We'll have him call you Tito," she said. He stiffened. He held his stomach as if he'd been sucker punched. "You want everyone to think your husband's the father?" "That would be best for the child, don't you think?"

At the hospital, watching her husband lovingly hug the baby against his cheeks in front of the family, Tomas immediately knew that he had made a grievous and irrevocable mistake. When Em was diagnosed with a metabolic disease, it had given Tomas the excuse to help out, taking Em to therapy and doctor's appointments: as he and Veronica were second cousins, her husband did not resist. For five years, he saw the boy at least twice a week. These moments with the boy were the parts of the week in which he replenished his soul.

He drove to the urgent care center. The Filipina nurse at check-in told them to get in line. Veronica pleaded with her to get Em to a doctor right away, and the nurse pursed her lips with tight annoyance, looking Veronica up and down as if deciding that this princess woman was used to getting preferential treatment just because of her beauty, an unfairness of the world, and I'll be damned if I'll follow that injustice.

Tomas stepped forward. "This boy needs to be put on an IV and hydrated, and some blood samples taken immediately of his carnitine and enzyme levels. I've got a letter from his pediatric neurologist, Dr. Wu, with details."

"Okay, give it to me and I'll show it to the doctor."

"No, we need to do this now. It explains it in the letter. He has a mitochondrial disease."

Her face looked blank. "A what?"

"It's a metabolic disorder. When he is overheated, as he seems to be now, he can go into metabolic breakdown."

"I don't know what that means."

"It means his body can't make enough energy to sustain life. It means he can have multiple organ failure, lung collapse, cardiac arrest. He can be taken from us. He can die. That is what is explained in this letter and which is why he needs to get that IV drip right away."

The nurse understood now, her eyes wide. Suddenly she was all urgency, nodding her head and hurrying her coworkers to find them a gurney where Em could be given a drip. As she pointed out portions of the letter to her colleagues and ordered people around, Tomas felt Veronica trembling beside him.

The nurse returned and gestured for them to follow. There had apparently been a school team bus accident and the hall was crowded with gurneys on which broken children waited for attention, and their family members looked up resentfully at Veronica and Tomas, with Em in his arms.

But the nurse ignored these indignant eyes and led them into a curtained partition and helped Tomas put the boy down on the gurney. A technician came in and readied some equipment.

It came time to put the first needle in. Em saw it and began to scream, trying to pull away, eyes wide in a last peak of sudden energy.

"Shhh, Em," Tomas said, stroking his hot hair, brushing his sweaty bangs off his forehead.

"I can't get the needle in," the technician said, with a frown. "He's kicking too much."

The boy arched and twisted.

The nurse looked at Veronica, hesitated, then continued to Tomas and said, "Come on, Dad. Help us."

He blushed in front of Veronica. But she nodded at him to go.

He stepped forward and smiled sweetly at the boy, then leaned over to hold him down. He hid the tumult in his own eyes and then voice as

147

he whispered gently in Em's ears, cupped the boy's small lovely head against his own cheek, drew courage from the image of his son lying lifeless on the gurney, his lips and eyelids blue and unmoving. He listened to the nurse and technician struggling to find a vein to put the needle in—knowing he would probably have to to do this again, and again, if he were lucky.

The doctor, when he came in, had a copy of the letter and read it over again several times while asking them about the details. He seemed impressed by the neurologist's name, and the words on the paper. He called neurology several times. They ran tests on Em's head, but found no cracks, no sign of concussion. He explained that the boy had probably gotten so upset that he worked himself into overheated exhaustion. But the boy seemed okay. They'd hold him overnight, but Tomas and Veronica should go out and get some food until Em got out of the current testing.

Veronica and Tomas walked out. In the parking garage she took his hand. Hers was trembling. They said nothing, but she turned and held him. She had not done this since that time, six years ago, they last made love beneath a blanket in a sand tent on Leo Cabrillo Beach, the wave rumble in the sand, knowing this would be their last time, the week they'd decided to part because it would be best if she and her husband raised the boy as their own. It had seemed the right thing to do then, if not right, though in the years following each time Tomas dropped the boy off and looked at the pattern of himself in Em's laughter and in his eyes, he regretted that decision with the searing certainty of physical pain.

Her body was warm. Her cheek hot against his chin. Her form slight in his hold. Her hip against his own. Her back felt warm on his cradling hand. She smelled good. She began to sob. They stood there for ten minutes, people coming out of the elevator and passing around them to their cars, until her sobs subsided to softness and her breathing eased back down to normal.

"Thank you," she said. She still held onto him.

"For what?"

"For carrying him to the car. For talking to that nurse so calmly. She hated me. She would have had us sit there while he went into organ failure."

"You wouldn't have let that happen."

"I would've sworn at her, made a scene, until the security guards came and threw me out. She'd made her mind up about me, that I was trying to get special treatment over other people's kids, that I felt entitled."

"Because you're pretty."

"So she thought," she said and held him. She hit his chest, still in his embrace, with a rebukeful half-smile. But she hit him hard. He lifted her chin and leaned in to kiss her. It lasted a moment, but he realized that her mouth was not moving, then her face turned aside.

They stood there quietly for a time. He felt the loss like a weight in his gut, or the lightness of a lost child. He could feel where she had hit him in the chest and jaw. Yet she kept holding him tight. He began to feel a shift, a subtle movement, as a child standing very still might sense the rotation of the earth. He waited for the right moment, felt it coming, the first real time in those six long years, to touch her chin and lift it to face him again. But then a van pulled into the disabled space beside them, its tires squealing to a sliding stop. It did not have disabled plates, and Veronica stiffened in his embrace. The woman who got out seemed in a hurry and glared at them as she approached the elevator. She walked on heels whose expensive leather straps stylishly entwined up her toned, slender calves. She bumped Veronica's side, though it would have been easy enough to step around.

"Excuse me," Veronica said.

The woman continued, hesitated, then turned to face them. "You shouldn't stand in the way like that. You were in my path. I'm in a rush."

"You don't have disabled plates."

"What?" The woman regarded them and something seemed to click in her mind. "You ought to mind your own business."

"That was the last spot."

The woman started to speak, but the elevator beeped and the door opened. She got on and shook her head with disgust as the doors swallowed her again.

Veronica stared at the closed chrome doors. Suddenly, she ran to the elevators and swung her purse at them and a metal part clicked against the chrome like change lost in tumbling laundry. Tomas went up and touched her shoulder, to stop her, but her muscles tightened.

She put her face in her hands and would not let him touch her.

He watched her. He waited, but still she did not move to let him close. He went over to the van. He double-checked the dash and rear-view mirror and both sets of plates, but did not see the familiar blue-and-white insignia he'd come to know so well these last few years. He knelt down near the left rear tire. He could smell the hot rubber, hear the clicks of the cooling underbody and tailpipe. He pulled out his pen-knife and slipped it in, his other palm on the warm rubber, listening to the tire's angry rebellious hiss as the chassis tipped and lowered toward the ground.

He turned around. The boy's mother was watching him. She had features from their son who lay in the hospital nearby and he tried to read her eyes.

The Carmelite

Dina had heard the story of her mother's legendary kidnapping many times, an event that happened back in the Philippines before the war.

Camille loved the rural family farm on which she spent her childhood summers, in a region of coconut groves and ocean-cooled mountains, the air scented by coconut husks being burned for charcoal. The rest of the year they lived in San Pablo. That is where she went to school. When she was sixteen her father entered her into a beauty contest and to her mortification she was chosen Miss Luzon. She proved popular and her photo was even printed on candy wrappers. The sassy *bakla* couturier was famed for his inventive eye and somehow made her look at once sophisticated and demure, Western and Asian, in elegant jazz age Maria Clara gowns with delicate lace touches and old-style butterfly sleeves. To her further horror, arrangements were made for Camille to tour the Philippines and several countries in Asia, to perform concert piano as she was taught by strict German nuns. Her father arranged for her to marry a man from a Visayan island family of sugarcane plantation money, so she ran away from home to a Carmelite nunnery near the coconut farm in Kawayan. She wished to be like her heroine, St. Teresa of Avila. And she yearned to live in the region of her beloved summer coconut farm. Here she could smell the bamboo-scented Quezon air. The convent was cloistered from the world, with high Spanish-era walls, surrounded by forests of bamboo that cupped the compound like caressing fingers. Her father came looking for her. She asked the nuns not to let him see her, so he went to the Bishop of Manila and the sisters had to allow a meeting.

Camille fretted over this information, begging the sisters not to let him see her, knowing her father's stubborn will and charismatic influence. She had heard the stories. A handsome man of Iberian charms, Santiago Navarro was legendary for having led guerrilla soldiers for Aguinaldo against first the Spanish, then the Americans (committing ambushes and atrocities against both), until the revolutionary president was captured by the treacherous deceptions of Gen. Funston, aided by Tagalog-hating Maccabebe Scouts, in 1902; Santiago felt the winds change and negotiated to switch sides to the Americans—in exchange for land.

The nuns took Camille down to the dusty courtyard where her large mestizo father waited among wandering chickens: Santiago Navarro wore a dapper white suit with a red pocket-handkerchief. Camille kept back, but the nuns nudged her forward. When she neared, her father reached out and grabbed her wrist—without a word—and began to drag her toward the front gate. She screamed. The Carmelites tried to hold onto her, clinging to her arms and legs and habit. But her father was huge and managed to drag them all to the front gate. Camille clasped the wrought iron, adorned with metal rose petals and thorns. She gripped so fiercely that her skin tore when he pried her off. Then he dragged her to his car. One of the sisters, a young novitiate, found her blood on an iron thorn; another noticed a bloody wound on her palm where the ornamentation had bitten in, just like the stigmata. They watched sadly as she looked out the back window with her sorrowful face, as her father's car pulled away and disappeared around a bend of banana trees.

She married the rich man from the Visayas, who gave her four children—Pepe, Ika, Betino and Dina—and then died and left her a widow at twenty-eight. He had not yet come into his inheritance and she would never receive it.

༒

Dina remembered returning to her mother's favorite "farm" during the Japanese Occupation, Navarro, a once great coconut hacienda of valleys and canyons and mountains that spread down to the azure bay, on which hundreds of tenant workers lived in villages. The once thriving operation was in ruins. The Japanese had burned the hacienda house down; typhoon rains and hot tropic sun rotted the remains, encroached on by jungle trees and vines. The family had so little food, Tia Checerida would slice a boiled egg into eleven parts for Dina and her siblings and cousins to share. But Camille seemed happy to be poor now, and preferred to pray in the simple thatch and woven nipa chapels the villagers built in the jungles. She and her sister Candida would visit with the local village women, and they adored her, slipped into the back pews simply to watch the famous beauty pray.

Over the decades Camille's story took on legendary character, though the woman never told it herself. She lived now in a tiny room at the back of Dina's modest Los Angeles apartment, dim and overlooking an alleyway with a view of a rusted gutter pipe. Camille prayed there for several hours a day. Dina's children and nieces and nephews could not believe that this old woman, still in mourning black and fat from eating leftovers off their plates (*she can't bear to see food go to waste—because we had none during the war*), had once been a beauty.

But her jazz age professional photographs told us otherwise. Still, we had reason to doubt the veracity of Filipino gossips. We heard her story from various people—distant aunts, family compadres, strangers. With each telling it was never quite the same. It traveled across family lines and continents, passed down generations, saved like candy wrappers kept tucked into family albums.

One afternoon we received a small box in the mail, from the Philippines, with a return address of a Carmelite nunnery in Quezon. Lola Camille was not at home, and my sister could not wait and decided to open it for her—against our protests. Inside, we found a white velvet blanket the size of a handkerchief, wrapped around a heavy object. It came apart carefully, like opening a flower. Inside, lay an iron rose petal, complete with stem and thorns.

ACKNOWLEDGMENTS

Most of the stories in this collection have changed over the years. Sometimes a basic concept or idea came from a snippet of half-heard anecdote, gossip, or legend, and I have been inspired by voices. But apart from a few references to historical figures, the characters and relationships that inhabit the stories are completely made up and do not resemble any living persons.

Some of these stories have drawn on material (characters, concepts, situations, themes, settings, and so on) originally published elsewhere and have since changed substantially. I'd like to thank the publications in which this material previously appeared, including *Ascent*, *American Literary Review*; *Mixed: An Anthology Short Fiction on the Multiracial Experience* (W. W. Norton); *Prairie Schooner*; *North American Review*; *Best Contemporary Filipino Novelists (Manila Envelope 4)*; *Growing Up Filipino 2* (edited by Cecilia Brainard); *The Seattle Review*; and the *Asian American Literary Review*. My gratitude to all the editors and staff of these publications not only for publishing the pieces but also for offering edits that helped them along their way.

One of those editors, Cecilia Brainard, has been particularly helpful with other aspects of this manuscript as well. My many thanks. Thanks also to Marianne Villanueva, who gave me advice on some of the stories. Other readers who have helped me with one or more stories include Drew Bennet, Jennifer Gilmore, Dan McCall, Maureen McCoy, Rafaelito Sy, Stephanie Vaughn, and Helena Maria Viramontes.

My great appreciation to Luisa Igloria, who was so helpful in editing the entire manuscript.

I'd like to give special thanks to Gianna Francesca Mosser, my immensely talented and energetic editor at Curbstone/Northwestern, who not only brought this book in but also shepherded me through the process and guided me through significant language, character, and structural edits to make it so much better.

Thanks to others at Northwestern University Press who also helped to make this book better and come to life, some unnamed to me but appreciated nonetheless. Including Nathan MacBrien for guiding it through edits, Jeanne Mrugacz, and of course Marianne Jankowski, the book's designer, for making it beautiful.

Thanks to my employer and colleagues at Miami University of Ohio for their support, including an essential leave. I worked on the book while on extended artist residencies at the Djerassi Resident Artists Program, the Virginia Center for the Creative Arts (VCCA), and Ragdale. Special thanks to Wolfson College and the University of Cambridge for providing essential support and resources during repeated stints, and where I finished the book.

To my maternal relatives: for teaching me to tell stories, and for your voices.

Thanks especially to my family. You helped me get through this. To my children, for your understanding when I have been writing away.

My lovely wife, Gwen, has been an especially honest and insightful reader over the years; thanks so much for your patience and support. I couldn't have written this without you.